THE ALABASTER HAND

(and other ghost stories)

by

A.N.L.Munby

THE ALABASTER HAND

First published by **Dennis Dobson Ltd** in 1949
This collection copyright © **Incunabul**a 2023

Stories copyright © **A.N.L.Munby**

Cover artwork copyright © **D M Mitchell**

www.incunabulamedia.com

ISBN 978-1-4478-6220-8

CONTENTS

Foreword

These stories were written between 1943 and 1945 in a prison-camp just outside the ancient walled town of Eichstätt in Upper Franconia. Three of them, 'The Four Poster', 'The White Sack' and 'The Topley Place Sale', appeared in *Touchstone,* a camp magazine; 'The Inscription' was first published in *Chambers' Journal.,* and 'The Devil's Autograph' in *The Cambridge Review.* The author is indebted to the editors of these periodicals for allowing them to be reprinted.

A. N. L. MUNBY

King's College,
Cambridge.
March 1949

HERODES
REDIVIVUS

I DON'T suppose that many people have heard of Charles Auckland, the pathologist, as he isn't the type of man who catches the public eye. What slight reputation he has got is of rather a sinister nature; for he has always tended to avoid the broad, beaten tracks of scientific research, and has branched off to bring light into certain dark cui-de-sacs of the human mind, which many people feel should be left unilluminated. Not that one would suspect it from his appearance. Some men who spend their lives studying abnormalities begin to look distinctly queer themselves, but not Auckland. To look at him one would put him down as a country doctor, a big red-faced man of about sixty, obviously still pretty lit, with a shrewd but kindly face. We belonged to the same club and for years had been on nodding terms, but I didn't discover until quite recently that he was a book collector and that only accidentally. I went to refer to Davenport's *Armorial Bookbindings* In the club library, and found him reading it. He deplored its inaccuracies, and I offered to lend him a list of corrections and additions that I had been preparing. This led to further discussion on bindings, and finally he invited me to go back with him to his flat and see his books. It was not yet ten o'clock and I agreed readily.

The night was fine, and we strolled together across the park to Artillery Mansions, where he was living at the time. On arriving we went up in the lift, and were soon seated in the dining-room of his flat, the walls of which were lined with books from floor to ceiling. I was glad to see that one alcove was entirely filled with calf and vellum bindings, the sight of which sent a little thrill of expectation down my spine.

I crossed the room to examine them, and my host rose too. A glance showed me that they were all of the class that second-hand booksellers classify comprehensively under the word 'Occult'. This, however, did not surprise me, as I knew of Auckland's interests. He took down several volumes, and began to expatiate on them - some first editions of the astrological works of Robert Fludd, and a very fine copy of the 1575 *Theatrum Diabolorum*. I expressed my admiration, and we began to talk of trials for witchcraft.

He had turned aside to fetch a copy of Scot's *Discoverie* to illustrate some point in his argument when suddenly my eye became riveted on the back of a small book on the top shelf, and my heart missed a beat. Of course it couldn't be, but it was fantastically like it! The same limp vellum covers without any lettering, with the same curious diagonal tear in the vellum at the top of the spine. My hand shook a little as I took it down and opened it. Yes, it was the book. I read once more the title villainously printed on indifferent paper: *Herodes Redivivus seu Liber Sclerosae Vitae et Mortis Sanguinolentae Rettzii, Monstri Nannetensis,* Parisiis, MDXLV. As I read the words memories came flooding back of that macabre episode which had overshadowed my schooldays. Some of the terror that had come to me twenty years before returned and I felt quite faint.

"I say, you must have a nose for a rarity," said Auckland, pointing to the volume in my hand.

"I've seen this book before," I replied.

"Really?" he said. "I'd be very glad to know where. There's no copy in any public collection in England, and the only one I've traced on the Continent is in the Ambrosian Library at Milan. I haven't even *seen* that. It's in the catalogue, but it's one of those books that librarians are very reluctant to produce. Can you remember where you've met it before?"

"I mean that I've seen this copy before," I answered.

He shook his head dubiously.

"I think you must be mistaken about that. I've owned this for nearly twenty years, and before that it was the property of a man that you're most unlikely to have met. In fact, he died in Broadmoor fifteen years ago. His name was…"

"Race," I interposed.

He looked at me with interest.

"I shouldn't have expected you to remember that," he said. "You must have been at school during the trial - not that it got much publicity. Thank God, there's legislation to prevent the gutter press from splashing that sort of stuff across their headlines." He half smiled. "You must have been a very precocious child - surely you were only a schoolboy at the time?"

"Yes," I replied. "I was a schoolboy - *the* schoolboy, one might say; the one who gave evidence at the trial and whose name was suppressed."

He put down the book he was holding and looked hard at me.

"That's most extraordinarily interesting. I suppose you wouldn't be willing to tell me about it? As you know, cases of that sort are rather my subject. Of course, it would be in the strictest confidence."

I smiled. "There's nothing in my story that I'm particularly ashamed of," I replied, "though I must confess that I occasionally feel that if I'd been a little more intelligent the tragedy might have been averted. However, I've no objection at all. It's only of academic interest now. I haven't thought about the matter for years.'

He sat me down in an armchair and poured me out a large whisky-and-soda, then settled himself opposite me.

3

"Take your time about it," he said. "I'm a very late bird and it's only a quarter to eleven.'

I took a long drink and collected my thoughts.

"I was at a large school on the outskirts of Bristol," I began, "and was not quite sixteen at the time of these events. Even in those days I was extremely interested in old books, a hobby in which I was encouraged by my housemaster. I never cut a great figure on the games field, and when it was wet or I was not put down for a game, I used to go book-hunting in Bristol. Of course, my purse was very limited and my ignorance profound, but I got enormous pleasure out of pottering round the shops and stalls of the town, returning every now and then with a copy of Pope's *Homer* or Theobald's *Shakespeare* to grace my study.

"I don't know whether you're acquainted with Bristol, but it's a most fascinating town. As one descends the hills towards the Avon, one passes from the Georgian crescents and squares of Clifton into the older maritime town, with its magnificent churches and extensive docks. Down by the river are many narrow courts and alleys, which are unchanged since the days when Bristol was a thriving medieval port. Much of this poorer area was out of bounds to the boys at school, but having exhausted the bookshops of the University area, I found it convenient to ignore this rule and explored every comer of the old town. One Saturday afternoon - it was in a summer term - I was wandering round the area between St Mary Redcliffe and the old 'Floating Harbour,' and I discovered a little court approached through a narrow passage. It was a miserable enough place, dark and damp, but a joy to the antiquarian - so long as he didn't have to live there! The first floors of the half-timbered houses jutted out and very nearly shut out the sky, and the court ended abruptly in a high blank wall. At the end on the right was a shop - at least the ground-floor window was filled with a collection of books. They were of little interest, and from the accumulation of dust upon them it was obvious that they hadn't been disturbed for years. The place had a deserted air, and it was in no great hope of finding it open that I tried the door. But it did open, and I found myself in its dark interior. Books were everywhere - all the shelves were blocked by great stacks of books on the floor with narrow lanes through which one could barely squeeze sideways, and over everything lay the same thick coating of dust that I'd noticed in the window. I felt as though I were the first person to enter it for years. No bell rang as I opened the door, and I looked round for the proprietor. I saw him sitting in an alcove at my right, and I picked my way through the piles of books to his desk. Did you ever see him yourself?"

"Only later in Broadmoor," replied Auckland. "I'd like you to describe in your own words exactly how he struck you at tile time."

"Well," I resumed, "my first impression of him was the extreme whiteness of his face. One felt on looking at him that he never went out into the sun. He had the unhealthy look that a plant gets if you leave a flower-pot over it and keep the light and air from it. His hair was long and straight and a dirty grey. Another thing that impressed me was the smoothness of his skin. You know how sometimes a man looks as though he has never had any need to shave - attractive in a young man but quite repulsive in an old one - well, that's how he looked. He stood up as I approached, and I saw he was a fat man, not grotesquely so but sufficiently to suggest grossness. His lips particularly were full and fleshy.

"I was half afraid of my own temerity in having entered, but he seemed glad to see me and said in rather a high-pitched voice, 'Come in, my dear boy; this is a most pleasant surprise. What can I do for you?'

"I mumbled something about being interested in old books and wanting to look round, and he readily assented. Shambling round from pile to pile, he set himself deliberately to interest me. And the man was a fascinating talker - in a very little while he had summed up my small stock of bibliographical knowledge and was enlightening me on dates, editions, issues, values and other points of interest. It was with real regret that I glanced at my watch and found that I had to hurry back to school. I had made no purchase, but he insisted on presenting me with a book, a nicely bound copy of Sterne's *Sentimental Journey,* and made me promise to visit him again as soon as I could."

"Have you still got the Sterne?' asked Auckland.

'No," I said, "my father destroyed it at the time of the trial. As the shop was in a part of the town that was strictly out of bounds, I didn't mention my visit to my housemaster, but on the following Thursday it was too wet for cricket and I returned to my newly found friend.

"This time he took me up to a room on the first floor, where there were more books and several portfolios of prints. Race, for such I discovered was his name, was a mine of information on the political history of the eighteenth century, and kept me enthralled by his exposition of a great volume of Gillray cartoons. The man had a sort of magnetism, and at that impressionable age I fell completely under his spell. He drew me out about myself and my work at school, and it was impossible for a boy not to feel flattered by the attention of so learned a man. It was easy to forget his rather repellent physical qualities when he talked so brilliantly.

"Suddenly we heard the shop door below opening, and with an exclamation of annoyance he descended the stairs to attend to the customer. A minute or two passed, and he did not return. I listened and could hear the murmur of conversation below. I idly pulled a book or two from the shelves and glanced at them, but there was little in the room that he had not already shown me. I went to the door and peered down over the stairs, but couldn't see what was going on. My ears caught a scrap of dialogue about the county histories of Somerset. I became bored. Across the landing at the top of the stairs was another room, the door of which was very slightly ajar. I'm afraid that I'm of a very inquisitive disposition. I pushed it open and peeped in. It was obviously where Race lived. There was a bed in one corner, a wardrobe, and a circular table in the middle of the room, but what caught my eye at once and held me spellbound was a picture over the fireplace. No words of mine can describe it."

Auckland nodded.

"I saw it - an unrecorded Goya - in his most bloodcurdling vein - made his *Witches' Sabbath* look like a school treat! It was burned by our unimaginative police force. They wouldn't even let me photograph it."

He sighed.

I resumed, "I went nearer to have a look at it. On the mantelpiece below it was a book - the book you've got now on your top shelf. I opened it and read the title page. Of course it meant nothing to me. Gilles de Retz doesn't feature in the average school curriculum. Suddenly I heard a noise behind me and swung round. There was Race standing in the doorway. He had come up the stairs without my hearing him. I shall never forget the blazing fury in his eyes. His face seemed whiter than ever as he stood there, a terrifying figure literally shaking with rage.

"I quickly tried to make my apologies, but he silenced me with a gesture; then he snatched the book from my hands and replaced it on the mantelpiece. Still without speaking, he pointed to the door and I went quickly down the stairs. He followed me down into the shop. I was about to leave without another word when suddenly his whole manner changed. It was as though he had recollected some powerful reason for conciliating me. He laid a hand on my arm.

"'My dear boy,' he said, 'you must forgive my momentary annoyance. I am a methodical man, and I can't bear people touching the things in my room. I'm afraid that living as something of a recluse has made me rather fussy. I quite realise that you meant no harm. There arc some very valuable books and pictures in there - not for sale, but my own private collection, and naturally I can't allow customers to wander in and out of it in my absence.'

"I expressed my contrition awkwardly enough, for the whole situation had embarrassed me horribly and I felt ill at ease. He perceived this and added, 'Now you mustn't worry about this - and least of all must you let it stop you coming here. I want you to promise that you'll visit me as soon as you can again - just to show that you bear no ill-will. I'll hunt out some interesting things for you to look at.'

"I gave him my promise and hurried back to school. In a day or two I had persuaded myself that I'd been imagining things, that some trick of the light had made him appear so distorted with rage. After all, why should a man get so angry about so little? As for the picture, it made comparatively little impression on my schoolboy mind. Much that it depicted was unintelligible to me at that time. I was, in any case, unlikely to be invited into the private room again. And so I resolved to pay a further visit to the shop.

"An opportunity didn't occur for nearly a fortnight, and when I did manage to slip down to Bristol, there was no mistaking how glad he was to see me. He was almost gushing in his manner. He had been as good as his word in finding more books to show me, and I spent a most pleasant after-noon. Race was as voluble as ever, but I got the impression that he was slightly distrait, as though he were labouring under some sort of suppressed excitement. Several times as I looked up from a book I caught him looking at me in a queer reflective way, which made me feel a little uncomfortable. When I finally said that I must go, he made a suggestion that he had never made before.

"'You've got very dusty,' he said. 'You really must wash your hands before you go. There's a basin downstairs - I'll turn on the light for you.'

"As he said this, he stepped across the shop, opened a door and turned a switch, illuminating a long flight of stairs. I descended them. They were of stone and led apparently into a cellar. As I reached the bottom step the light was extinguished. I turned sharply and saw him standing at the head of the stairs - a fantastic, foreshortened figure at the top of the shaft, silhouetted in the doorway. He had his hands stretched out, holding on to the jambs of the door, and with the half-light of the shop behind him he looked like a misshapen travesty of a cross. I called out to him and started to remount the stairs, but as I did so he quickly closed the door without saying a word.

"I was terribly afraid. Of course, it might have been a joke but I knew inside me that it wasn't and that I was in the most deadly peril. I reached the top of the stairs and groped at the door, but there seemed to be no handle inside. I couldn't find the switch either; it must have been in the shop. I shouted.

9

There was no reply. An awful horror gripped me the dank smell of the stone cellar; the lack of air and the darkness, all conspired to undermine what little courage I possessed. I shouted again, then listened holding my breath. All at once I heard the outer shop door open and an unfamiliar footstep inside the shop. With all my strength I pounded on the door, shouting and screaming like a madman. The noise reverberating round the confined space nearly deafened me. I listened again for a second; voices were raised in the shop, but I caught no words. I shouted again until I felt my lungs would burst and hammered on the door until my fists were bruised. Suddenly it was flung open and I stumbled out, hysterical with fear and half blinded by the daylight. Before me stood an old clergyman, behind him Race, who bore on his face the same look of malevolent fury that I bad seen before.

"'What is the matter?' asked the clergyman. 'How did you get shut in there?'

"It was then that I made my fatal mistake. All I wanted was to get away and never come back again. If I lodged a complaint, I foresaw endless trouble, with the school authorities, even with the police. My terror had evaporated with the daylight, and I was feeling more than a little ashamed of myself.

"'I went down to wash my hands,' I said. 'The lights went out and I got frightened. I'm quite all right now, though.'

"The clergyman looked enquiringly at Race, but the latter had recovered his self-possession.

"'The lights must have fused,' he said; 'they often do - it's the damp. I was just going to let him out when you came in. No wonder he was frightened. It's a most eerie place in the dark.'

"The clergyman looked from him to me, as if inviting some

comment from me, but I merely said, 'I ought to be getting back to school now.'

"We left the shop together, and as we walked through the passage out of the court I looked back, and there was Race standing on the step of his shop following us with baleful eyes. My companion seemed to be debating whether he would ask me a question, but he refrained. I hardly liked to ask him to say nothing about the episode; he obviously wished to satisfy his curiosity, but we were complete strangers and, though old enough to be my grandfather, he seemed to be a diffident man. It was a curious relationship.

"He put me on to a bus, and I thanked him gravely. As we shook hands he said abruptly, 'I shouldn't go there again,' and turned away.

"For a few days I was on tenterhooks lest he should make any report of the occurrence to the school, but as the days became weeks and I heard no more, my mind became at rest. I had firmly decided that nothing would induce me to visit Race's shop again and soon the whole episode assumed an air of unreality in my mind."

I looked at my watch.

"Good Lord!" I said to Auckland, "it's getting pretty late. Do you want to go to bed? We could have another session tomorrow."

"Certainly not," he replied. "I find your story of the most absorbing interest. It fills in all sorts of gaps in my knowledge of the affair. If you don't mind sitting up, I should greatly appreciate it if you'd carry on."

He refilled my glass and I settled myself more comfortably into my chair.

"Well," I continued, "I'm a bit diffident about telling the rest of the story. Up to now it's been pretty strange, but it has been sober fact; now we get into realms where I find myself a bit out of my depth."

Auckland nodded.

"Never mind," he said, "Let's have it. Just as it comes back to you - don't try to explain it, just tell me what happened."

"A year passed and I was still at school," I continued. "I'd got into the Sixth Form and was working pretty hard for a scholarship. I'd also got into the House Cricket XI by some miracle, and so I couldn't be so free-and-easy about games as I had been previously. Public opinion forced me to take them fairly seriously. A dropped catch at a critical point in a match can make a schoolboy's life pretty good hell.

"At that age I used to sleep extraordinarily well – I still do for that matter. It was very rare for me to dream and then only of trivial affairs. But on the night of June 26th - I noted the date in my diary - I had me first of a couple of particularly horrible dreams. I dreamed most vividly that I was back in Race's shop. Every detail of that untidy interior passed in an accurate picture through my brain. I was standing in the middle of the shop, and it was dusk. Very little light came through those dusty windows piled high with books. Race himself was nowhere to be seen. The door to the cellar which had such sinister associations for me was closed. Suddenly from the other side of it came a series of appalling screams and shouts, intermingled with muffled bangs and thumps on the door. I ran across and tried to open it, but it was locked. Then I darted out to the shop steps to see if anyone was at hand to assist me, but the court was deserted. I stood irresolute in the shop, and then all at once the cries seemed to get weaker and the banging on the door ceased. I listened and could hear the sounds of a struggle on the stairs gradually getting fainter as it reached the cellar below.

"At this point I awoke shivering with fright, bathed in a cold sweat. Sleep was impossible for me during the rest of the night. I lay and thought about my dream. It seemed so queer that I should dream, not of my own experience on the stairs, but from the point of view of an observer.

"The next night exactly the same thing occurred, and the horror of the scene so impressed me that I must have cried out in my sleep, for I found that I'd awakened several of the other boys in my dormitory. I couldn't bear the anticipation of having such a dream a third time and I went to the House Matron on the following day and told her that I couldn't sleep. She moved me from the dormitory into the sick-room and gave me a sedative. On that night and thereafter I slept quite normally again.

"Not quite a fortnight later a further link was forged in this extraordinary chain of events. I was passing the local police station and I stopped to read a notice posted outside about the protection of wild birds - I've always been a bit of an ornithologist. Along the railings in front of the building were hung the usual medley of notices - Lost, Found and Missing. My eye caught one more recent than the others - and I idly read it.

"I cannot, of course, remember the exact wording at this date, but it asked for information about a boy named Roger Weyland, aged fifteen and a half. He was described in detail, and I remember being struck at once by his similarity to myself. He had left his home at Clevedon after lunch on June 26th to bicycle into Bristol, where he intended to visit the docks. He was last seen near St Mary Redcliffe at about half - past five the same afternoon, and the police were asking anyone to come forward who could throw light on his whereabouts.

"I read and reread the notice. Its implication dawned on me at once. It's no good asking why, but I assure you that at the moment I *knew* what had happened. My dream of the night of June 26th was still fresh in my memory, and even in the broad sunlit street I shuddered and was oppressed by a feeling of nameless horror.

"I debated what I should do. The police, I felt sure, would laugh at me. I could never bring myself to walk into the station and blurt out such a fantastic tale to some grinning sergeant. But I must tell someone; and after dinner that day I sought an interview with my housemaster. He was a most understanding man, and listened in patient silence while I told him the whole story. I must have spoken with conviction, because at the end of it he rang up a friend of his, a local Inspector of Police. Half an hour later I repeated my tale to him. He was very polite, asked one or two searching questions, but I could see that he was sceptical. He did, however, agree with my housemaster that Race's activities might profitably be looked into.

"If you followed the trial, I suppose you know all the rest; how they found the boy's body and God-knows-what other devilish things beside. My name was suppressed in the evidence, and I left school at the end of that term and went abroad for six months.

"One very odd thing about it all was that they never traced the clergyman. The police were most anxious to get him to corroborate my story, and my father was equally keen to find him - after all, he saved my life - and my father wanted to show some tangible appreciation of the fact, subscribe generously to one of his favourite charities or something. It's very queer really that the police, with their entire nation-wide organisation, never got on to him. After all, there aren't a limitless number of clergymen, and the number of those in the Bristol area that afternoon must have been comparatively small. Perhaps he didn't like to come forward and be connected with such a business, but I don't think that's very likely - he didn't strike me as the sort of man who would shirk his obligations.

"That's really all that I can tell you, and I expect you knew some of that already."

"A certain amount," replied Auckland, "but by no means all. I occasionally get asked questions by the police in this kind of case and I did assist them on this occasion, though I wasn't called in evidence. Race had a damned good counsel in Rutherford, and managed to convince the jury that he was insane. If a man is sufficiently wicked, a British jury will often believe that he must be mad. And so he went to Broadmoor. Of course, he was as sane as you and I are."

"How did you come to get hold of one of his books?" I asked.

"Through the good offices of the police," he said. "Perhaps as a sort of consolation prize for my distress at the destruction of the Goya. The book is really the clue to Race. It is a contemporary account of the activities of Gilles de Retz, Marshal of France, hanged at Nantes in 1440. I expect you know a certain amount about him; he figures in all the standard works on Diabolism. The contemporary authorities are a bit vague on the exact number of children he murdered. Monstrelet says a hundred and sixty, but Chastellain and some others put it at a hundred and forty. But all this is general knowledge.

"What isn't so widely known is that every now and then he seems to reappear in history - at least the devilish practices, with which his name is associated, crop up again and again.

He was quite a cult in seventeenth-century Venice, and there was a case in Bohemia in the middle of the last century. A variant of de Retz's name is de Rais and Race himself claimed to be a descendant; but I've no proof of this. The police failed to trace his parentage or to find any details about him before he appeared in Bristol just before the First World War. His shop has gone now; the whole of that area was pulled down in a recent slum-clearance scheme.

"The trial at Nantes in 1440 has always been an interest of mine, and I had a great find the last time I was in Paris. Some early Nantes archives had recently been acquired by the Bibliotheque Nationale, and   I spent   a happy week examining all   the original   documents   relating to the examination of the woman, La Meffrie, who procured most of the children for de Retz. I've got transcripts of the most important. Would you care to borrow them? They are quite enthralling."'

"Not on your life," I replied as I rose to take my leave. "I came far too near to playing the principal role to read about such things with any pleasure. You may be able to take a detached, scientific view of the ease, but, believe me, I've had ·enough of de Retz and all his works to last me a lifetime."

THE
INSCRIPTION

The Knowledge that Charles Winchcombe had a good working library at his house in Dorset drove away any twinges of conscience that I might have had about leaving London. I was working against time preparing a paper for the journal of a certain learned society, and for the last ten days I had been busy at the British Museum. It had been stifling hot, and my subject – Cluniac Foundations in South Wales - demanded more concentration than I could give it with the temperature at ninety in the shade. Charles' invitation to spend a weekend with him was more than welcome under the circumstances, and I hastened to send him a wire announcing my arrival that evening.

Stapton Manor is one of the most delightful small houses that I know. It is not a show-place in any sense of the word, and in that perhaps lies its charm. It is not a perfect specimen of any one period or style; it has grown almost insensibly during four centuries. A Tudor shell, extended in the seventeenth century, had been 'modernised' about 1745 by the addition of a small Palladian façade. A late eighteenth century owner had impaired the symmetry by building on a further wing, but the assemblage was wholly pleasing.

Such was the haven that I reached by the four-forty-five from Paddington. Charles was at the station himself and greeted me warmly. I had known him for years. We were at Cambridge together, and I had kept up with him ever since. I had a great affection for Charles, though our tastes were in many ways dissimilar. He was an ardent sportsman, and much of his time was spent in superintending the affairs of his estate. He did not share my antiquarian interests; indeed, I was sometimes a little shocked at how much he took for granted his perfect house. He was, in fact, a representative of that dying class, the country squire, who could still afford to maintain the establishment of his ancestors.

His wife, Mary, I had known even longer - for she had been an old friend of my sister's and had stayed with us as a child. I used to get a certain amount of quiet amusement out of comparing the graceful, self-possessed mistress of Stapton with the rather shy, gawky girl that I remembered in the old days. I knew them quite well enough to explain that I had brought down some work to finish, and that I should want to shut myself up in the library for a few hours every day. Charles twitted me rather ponderously about my subject, but they both agreed readily enough.

On the following day I put in a really good morning's work, and I felt pretty pleased with myself at lunch-time. After we had had our coffee Charles suggested a stroll round the gardens. We stood for a moment on the terrace at the back of the house, looking down to the lake and the wooded hillside beyond it. On this glorious afternoon it seemed extraordinarily beautiful. We walked towards the lake, talking of commonplaces.

After a while Charles said, "By the way, I don't think I told you that I'm pulling down the old temple on the island. Not that it needs much pulling down - it's been in a terrible state for years." He appeared to sense the protest which was on the tip of my tongue, for he went on, "It's never struck me as being a thing of beauty- you can't see it from the house, or from any other viewpoint for that matter. And the stone will come in useful for the new barn at the home farm. The men were demolishing it this morning. Let's go and see how they're getting on."

We walked along the edge of the lake, following a narrow arm or it that ran into a strip of woodland. The trees came right down to the bank, casting their shade over the water, which looked black and forbidding. Even then it seemed to be a most cheerless corner of the property. A small rustic bridge led onto the island. It was a tiny place, overgrown with ground-ivy, hollies and evergreens. At the far side in a little hollow stood the temple, a stone building of the sort that our ancestors in the eighteenth century loved to scatter about their grounds. It was not a particularly good example of its kind; a perfectly plain rectangular building with an open front, composed of a plain pediment on four little Doric columns. When I considered it, this did seem a curious place to have erected such a building. As my friend said, it was invisible to anyone not actually on the island I wondered what eccentric whim had prompted a man to build it in such a very inaccessible and gloomy spot.

I could not see any very substantial reason against demolishing the temple, though I felt that, as a good antiquary, it was incumbent on me to make some sort of protest.

"Don't you think it's rather a pity not to let it stay here?" I asked rather half-heartedly. "I'm sure you can get the stone elsewhere for the barn. After all, this has been here since 1769."

"Why 1769? As a matter of fact, it's later than that. It wasn't built until 1785. There's a drawing in the gun-room showing it when it was newly erected."

"I think you must be mistaken," I said. "Look at this." I pointed to a portion of the lintel of the partially demolished entrance. One end had been broken away, but incised upon it, quite plainly, were the letters CCL.X.IX. "That must once have read MDCCLXIX," I urged. "I presume the rest of the lintel is somewhere around."

We looked about among the heaps of rubble, but couldn't see it.

"I expect that it's gone off with the first load," Charles remarked. "It's queer that it's dated 1769. I could almost swear the inscription on the drawing says 1 785. We must look when we get back to the house. But whatever the date was, it's coming down. No one sees it from one year's end to another. And the stone really will be useful - the local quarry has closed down and I should have to go miles for it otherwise. Some of the wood is quite sound, too." He kicked a beam from the roof which lay on the ground at our feet. "Well, we must be getting back. Davis, my agent, is coming in after tea."

When we had recrossed the bridge 1 looked back at the island. I thought I saw a sign of movement in the dark clump of laurel bushes, as though some animal were concealed there, but when I pointed it out to Charles the movement ceased.

After tea we looked at the drawing in the gun-room. Charles had been quite right. An inscription read; 'The Temple erected and dedicated in the year 1785 by Samuel Winchcombe, Esq., of the Manor of Stapton in the County of Dorset.'

I noticed the artist's initials G. L. in one corner, but Charles could throw no light on his identity. We reverted to the date.

"Perhaps the dated lintel is a stone from some older building," I suggested. "It's odd, though, that it should have been used in such a prominent place."

"It's much more likely that either the engraver of the stone or the artist made a mistake," replied Charles; and I agreed that this was the most probable reason for the discrepancy.

"Do you know much about Samuel Winchcombe?" I asked.

"Surely I've told you about him?" he replied. "My wicked

ancestor - the skeleton in the cupboard."

"No, I 'm sure you haven't. I should have remembered. Tell me."

"Well," he said, "there isn't much to tell. He was really rather a pathetic figure. An eccentric and a recluse, he lived alone in this house except for one manservant. He never left the grounds or allowed anyone to enter the park, and he was never known to go to church - not, at least, until he died in 1795. I've seen his tomb in the family vault. My great grandfather, who was his nephew, inherited the place. As you can imagine it was in an appalling stale; for over twenty years nothing had been done in the way of repairs, and the gardens hadn't been touched. In fact, the only piece of building done in his time was that ridiculous temple. It took *my* great-grandfather ten years to get the place into order. It was he who added the west wing.

"You can imagine the sort of gossip that a man like Samuel Winchcombe aroused in a country place. Every sort of horror was ascribed to him by the local people, without, apparently, any justification. I think he went the pace a bit as a younger man - he used to stay a lot at Medmenham in the 1760s. He may have dabbled in the occult in a dilettante sort of way; it was a fashionable folly at that time. But I've never discovered anything particularly discreditable about him. Apart from his neglect of the estate, I should think he was a most harmless old man.

"There was one unfortunate occurrence while he lived here. A gipsy was found drowned in the lake, and, of course, all the villagers said at once that he had been murdered. There was never the slightest evidence for such a statement, but you can't stop country people from manufacturing slanderous rumours. I expect all this talk reached the cars of the old man, for after

21

that he was more of a recluse than ever. Have you seen his portrait? It's up in the attic over the west wing. It used to hang in the hall when I was a boy, but Mary didn't like it. You know how silly women are sometimes about things like that!"

I had never seen the picture and we mounted the stain to the attic. It was the usual country-house lumber-room, full of the fascinating bric-a-brac that accumulates in an old mansion. In one corner was a stack of pictures and prints. Charles looked through them, and pulling one out, set it in the light near the window.

"There you are" he said. "He isn't a beauty, *is* he?"

The figure portrayed was that of a very old man – very old and very evil-looking. I expect you know Houdon's statue of Voltaire - well, it reminded me very much of that. The same seated figure hunched forward in the chair, with two claw-like hands clutching the arms, the same skull-like head sunk between the shoulders. But there the resemblance ended. The latent humour that lurks in the face of Houdon's statue was entirely lacking in the picture. It lacked, too, the humanity in the face of the venerable philosopher. I didn't wonder that Mary had wanted it moved - indeed, marvelled that Charles himself could be so insensitive to the malevolent spell that it seemed to cast upon the spectator.

"It's a most powerful piece of painting," I said. "Do you know the artist?"

"It was painted by the old man's servant," he answered.

"He was an Italian and had been trained as an artist in his boyhood. Now that I come to think about it, it may have been the same man who made the drawing of the temple."

He replaced the picture in the stack, and we went downstairs. I don't think that anything further happened that week-end which has any bearing on this narrative. I made good progress with my paper and returned to London on Tuesday morning with the greater part of my work completed.

It was a great shock for me to see the notice of Charles's death in *The Times* about a month later. Apart from the fact that he had met with an accident, the announcement told me nothing. I couldn't get down to the funeral, but, of course, I wrote to Mary at once. She replied by return of post, and from her letter I learned that Charles had fallen off the scaffolding while inspecting the new barn.

She ended by saying, "If you are free, I would be so glad if you could come down for a few days. There are all sorts of points on which I want advice, and you are such a very old friend of both Charles and myself. I really don't feel up to coping with things at present, and you could take such a lot of minor worries off my hands…"

Needless to say I went at once. Poor Mary had obviously had a great shock but she was bearing up bravely. She was more human and tender than I'd known her to be for years. Charles's death had temporarily shattered her serenity and her poise, and she was far less the grand lady than she had been.

After tea the butler asked me if I would see Davis, the agent, who was waiting in the library. I joined him in a few minutes. I had, of course, met him before on previous visits, a pleasant man of something over thirty, the son of a local doctor. He looked worried as he rose to greet me.

"I'm so glad that you've come down," he said. "There's something very much on my mind, which I didn't feel I could discuss with Mrs Winchcombe. The morning after Mr. Winchcombe's death I went up to the house to look for some documents connected with the estate, leases that I'd left with him to sign. On his desk I happened to see his diary, and as I knew that he'd made several appointments in connection with buying two new farms, I thought I would take a note of them. I'd often done such a thing before, with his permission. I know that I shouldn't have pried about among a dead man's papers, but the estate work has to go on as usual, and the arrangements for buying these two farms were in a very advanced state.

"Anyhow - on opening his diary I couldn't help reading a very curious entry, so curious that I felt justified in taking the book away with me. I have a great admiration for Mrs. Winchcombe, and I knew that if she were to read the diary it would only give her unnecessary distress. Mr Winchcombe was usually a most sane, well-balanced man, but from what he has written down it would appear that he was suffering from some sort of nervous disorder before he died - some sort of hallucinations. People might even say that he committed suicide if some of these entries were made public. I do so hope that you'll think I did right, because it's been very much on my conscience. I've got the book here, and would like you to look through it - just the last month before the accident. Then you can advise me on what I ought to do with it."

I took the diary and promised to see him on the following day. At dinner I said nothing of this interview, but we discussed Mary's future. She told me that for the present things would go on as before. I knew that Charles had been a rich man and that she was well provided for.

Going off to my room as early as I could, I settled down to Charles's diary. It was, in general, a very normal day-to-day record of events, notes of appointments, interviews with his agent, his head-keeper, and tenants. Then, as I read, an abnormal note began to creep into the entries - the first sign of it was three weeks before his death. I will set the relevant passages down;

"*September 2nd.* I had an odd experience tonight. Walking back from the lake, I saw what I thought was a figure hiding in the rhododendrons on the left of the path. Thinking that perhaps it was a poacher, I walked over to investigate, but there was nothing there. I suppose it was some stupid trick of the light.

"*September 4th.* I again thought I saw a man by the lake, this time by the boathouse. I couldn't sec him clearly. I must tell Jackson (the head-keeper) to post someone down there in the evening to try to catch him. Haven't mentioned this to Mary.

"*September 5th.* I was followed home tonight. I *know* I was. I could hear footsteps rustling in the grass behind me, but whenever I turned my head they stopped. It was like playing that children's game Grandmother's Steps with some invisible creature. Perhaps I ought to see a doctor. I shan't go out in the evening for a bit.

"*September 8th.* I did a thing tonight that I haven't done for thirty years. I looked under the bed and in the cupboards before turning in. Cod knows what I expected to find. I'm getting awfully jumpy. I try not to let Mary notice it.

"*September 10th.* I was up at the home farm today and had climbed up a ladder to see how the building was going. There was hardly a breath of wind, but when 1 got to the top and was standing on the wall, a sudden gust caught me and very nearly blew me off. I felt just as though I'd received a sharp push in the small of the back. Luckily I managed to grasp one of the roof joists and saved myself from falling. It was a most unpleasant experience... The vicar this afternoon said that I wasn't looking very well and I nearly told him all about my experience, but I couldn't bring myself to do so. I hate looking a fool. Anyhow, we're going off to Scotland in a fortnight's time. I shan't be sorry."

For the next week my poor friend's entries were quite normal. Indeed, he remarked that 'he felt much better and was sleeping more soundly,' and on another occasion that he 'couldn't think why he'd been so off-colour the previous week.'

The last entry was innocent enough in itself, but ominous in the light of subsequent events.

"*September 19th.* Davis in this evening, and I arranged to meet him at the home farm at 10:00 a.m. tomorrow. The barn is nearly completed and by all accounts a very good job. I must inspect it thoroughly..."

On the following day Charles had met with his fatal accident. The words written by the dead man made a deep impression on me, the more so as I knew that he was the personification of robust common sense, a stolid and unimaginative man if ever there was one. I fully agreed with Davis that Mary should be spared from knowledge of her husband's strange nervous disorder. I decided to see him as early as I could on the following morning and recommend the destruction of the diary and a bond of silence about the affair.

After breakfast I set out to walk to the estate office. Before I had got half-way I met Davis hurrying up towards the house.

"Thank heaven, I've met you," he said. "Something rather odd has happened. Come down to the lake with me and I'll tell you about it on the way." We turned off down the hill together. "I've still kept one labourer digging out the foundations of the temple on the island," he continued, "and he has just found that there's a vault underneath it, with a coffin in it. As soon as I heard about it, I came up to fetch you.

I've told him to keep quiet meantime." We walked through the dark strip of woodland and crossed the little bridge onto the island.

An old countryman with a spade touched his hat and stood aside. It was only a shallow vault, containing a single plain lead coffin. There appeared to be no inscription upon it. It did not quite fill the vault, and I peered down into the spaces at the ends. Something caught my eye and, kneeling down, I pulled it out. It was a small glass phial of cylindrical shape, sealed at the mouth. It was covered with mildew and filth, but I could dimly discern inside it what looked like a paper.

I took out my knife and worked away at the seal. Whoever had fastened it up had done his work well. At last the stopper came cleanly away, and I drew out a vellum document, tightly rolled up. It had suffered a little from the damp, but was still quite legible. I spread it out and Davis and I pored over it together.

'Directions for the Burial of Samuel Winchcombe, arranged with his servant Giovanni Leoni on the 17th day of March, 1787. The Directions to be laid with him in his grave.

'In so far as there be certain cogent Reasons why my Body shall not be interred in Ground that is by some called Holy I do direct that upon my Death my servant Giovanni Leoni shall secretly bring my Body by Night to the Temple which I have prepared for it upon the Island, and which I have dedicated to certain Divinities with all Solemnity and Ceremony, even having brought about the Death of a wandering Gipsy Man for their Gratification. And lest there be a Public Clamour at such an Irregularity I do direct that an empty Coffin bearing my Name upon it shall be interred in the Parish Church of St. Peter, *as* though I had been a Christian

27

man. And to safeguard my Bones from Insult and my Resting Place from Desecration I have posted a Sentinel there who will be swift to take vengeance upon any Possessor of the Manor of Stapton foolhardy enough to disregard the Instruction that I have set plainly for all to see. For over the Doorway I have set a Text from the Book which the Unenlightened call Sacred. And woe betide him that shall ignore it.

'Samuel Winchcombe

'Laus Principi Aeris.'

Davis and I looked at each other in silence. The same thoughts went through our minds. He was the first to speak. Turning to the old man, he said, "This is the grave of an ancestor of Mr. Winchcombe's. We must cover it up again carefully. I particularly want to avoid distressing Mrs. Winchcombe so soon after her husband's accident, and I want you to promise that you won't speak of this to anyone. We don't want a lot of gossip and talk at a time like this."

The old man looked at him steadily and replied slowly, "I won't tell no one."

Without another word he bent to his task of putting back the stone slabs which covered the vault. We helped him to lower them into place and left the island together. Davis gave him instructions to return later and remove the little bridge, thus isolating the island with its sinister secret from the mainland.

As we walked back up the hill I enquired about the old man. "Is he reliable? Will be really keep his mouth shut?"

"His family has been on the estate for three generations," Davis replied. "If old Thomas Baker says be won't mention a thing, you can take it that the secret is safe. Thank God, it was he and not one of the younger men."

We talked the matter over in the library of the house, and

agreed that during Mary Winchcombe's lifetime we should never speak of our strange discoveries. Her death a month ago leaves me at liberty to recount this strange history. We burned the diary and the document from the grave. Before we did so, we reread the parchment.

"What does it mean when it says 'Over the doorway I have set a text'?" asked Davis.

A text! I wrote down from memory the inscription CCL.X.IX. What a fool I had been! There were no stops in a Roman date. Of course, the missing letter must have been E - Eccl. x. ix.

I quickly turned up the passage in a Bible and read, "Whoso removeth stones shall be hurt therewith; and he that cleaveth wood shall be endangered thereby."

THE ALABASTER
HAND

"Can you come and stay night advice urgently needed Travers Vicarage Brandon St. Giles."

I read the prepaid telegram with some surprise. I could think of no subject on which Cecil Travers would want my advice. However, I sent off the reply, promising to be with him by tea-time, and resumed my interrupted reading of *The Times*. But I found it very difficult to concentrate, and found myself constantly reverting to the problem of why Cecil Travers should have sent me this urgent summons. It wasn't as though I knew him very well; in fact, I hadn't seen him at all since his father's death, a couple of years before.

His father had been my Contemporary at Cambridge, and I had taken a mild interest in the boy's career. Not that he was a boy now - he must have turned thirty. He certainly wouldn't want to consult me on any matter of business. Such things were definitely not in my line. Cecil Travers represented for me muscular Christianity at its best. At Cambridge he had combined a very poor degree with a Rugger Blue - in fact, he was one of the best wing forwards that the University had produced since the war. He had always been destined for the Church, and after his ordination had put in eight years as a curate in a poor parish in Bristol. Here his success was in a large measure due to his occasional appearances on the football field. As he himself was the first to admit, the tries he scored on Saturday afternoon brought far more people to church than ever his sermons did. About nine months ago he had been presented to the living of Brandon St Giles, about ten miles from Norwich.

Three o'clock on a Monday afternoon in November found

me approaching the village. I was filled with a pleasant sense of well-being. The Daimler had brought me down in excellent time, and as I neared the end of my journey I slackened *my* pace and looked about me. East Anglia never appealed to me very much, and certainly Travers had settled in a bleak corner of it. The cold, Oat landscape, with the mist already beginning to rise, accentuated the warmth of the car's interior. I breasted a slight rise in the road and the little village of Brandon St. Giles lay before me. It wasn't much of a place, a few outlying farms were discernible to the right and left, and straight ahead was a small cluster of cottages, three shops and one or two small Georgian houses fronting on to the road. The only notable feature of the village was its church, and like so many East Anglian churches its size was out of all proportion to the small, community which it served. The wealth of the wool trade had obviously built it in the fifteenth century – a splendid example of the Perpendicular style - and it still remained as a reminder of the days when farmers could become men of substance in a generation. Beyond it lay the vicarage, and I pulled in at the little drive that led up to the pleasant stone-built house. A maid answered my ring, and showed me into the drawing-room, where a log fire was burning brightly.

"The vicar is just getting up, sir," she said. "He'll be down directly." This was the first intimation I had that my friend had been ill, and I asked the maid how long he'd been in bed.

"He was taken queer at the service last night," she replied, "but he's much better today."

Our conversation was interrupted by the entrance of my host, who apologised for not having been up to receive me.

"It's extremely kind of you to have come so quickly," he said, dismissing the maid with a gesture. "I do hope that you

31

won't think that I've brought you here on a wild-goose chase, but knowing your interest in…", he hesitated, "…well, what you'd call the supernatural, I thought I'd like to get your opinion on a very odd experience I had yesterday evening. That's what upset me."

I looked at him. He didn't have his normal healthy colour.

"Of course any advice that I can give is at your disposal," I said. "Let me hear about it."

He glanced at his watch.

"I'd like to take you over to the church first," he answered. "before it gets dark. We've time before tea."

We crossed the vicarage garden, and passed through a doorway in the wall which led directly into the churchyard. Travers led the way along a path between the graves which skirted the buttressed north wall. We entered the vestry door at the east end and emerged into the choir. On both sides the finely carved choir-stalls ran right up to the altar steps. Travers faced the altar and indicated - with some hesitancy I thought - a tomb let into a recess in the wall on the right of it.

"What do you think of that?" he said.

I examined the monument closely. On the flat slab covering the tomb was a recumbent alabaster effigy, wearing the gown and bands of a priest. It was a finely executed piece, the face in particular, which was aquiline and ascetic. The arrangement of the hands and arms was unusual - in fact, unique in my experience. Instead of being clasped across the bosom or placed together upon the breast in the conventional attitude of prayer, one hand was tucked into a fold in the gown, whilst the other, the one nearest to me, was stretched out at an angle, projecting over the edge of the slab upon which the figure lay. The hand pointed towards the altar. The choir-stalls bad obviously been built after the monument, and the top stall of the row was almost hard up against the tomb, enclosing it in a dark, sunless alcove.

"It's very fine," I said, "and in extraordinarily good condition. I suppose its rather inaccessible position has preserved it."

"What do you think of the epitaph?" he asked, pointing to a deeply incised Latin inscription on the side of the tomb. I examined it and translated:

'Here lies the body of Walter Hinkman, born in the year of Our Lord 1470, who departed this life on the 27th of April 1536. For thirty years he performed the duties of Vicar in this parish of Brandon St. Giles, well beloved by his flock. This monument was erected in the year of Our Lord 1538 by his successor John Melcombe, formerly of the Charterhouse.'

Below was a hexameter:

EN! MANUS AETERNOS VENERANDA EST
SANCTA PER ANNOS.

And I rendered it as: "Lo! It is meet that the company of the saints should be honoured through eternity."

"How did you translate *Sancta Manus*?" asked Travers.

"The *sacred band* - the company of the Saints." I replied.

"You don't think *Manus* is used in its sense of hand?" he answered.

"Of course it could mean *holy hand*," I said, "but it seems extremely unlikely. I can't see what it could indicate."

"Well, the hand of the effigy is very prominent, isn't it?" he said dubiously. "What do you make of the figure itself?"

"It's a good specimen of a not very uncommon class of post Reformation alabaster work," I answered. "Do you know the effigy of Bishop Sherburne at Chichester? That's about the same date, but more elaborate, of course."

Travers shook his head. "I'm no antiquary," he said. "I was

too busy playing games as a boy, and I defy anyone who's a curate in a slum parish to find time for archaeological studies. Is there anything else odd about it?"

"I don't think so," I said, "apart from the arrangement of the arms, which I don't think I've seen elsewhere. Of course, it's a costly monument for a parish priest, but I know of several others just as elaborate; there is a fine one at Wilmslow in Cheshire, for example."

I was beginning to lose interest in the matter.

"Will you show me round the church?" I said. "I've heard you've some pretty good glass."

"Tommorow morning," he said hastily. "We'd better get back to tea now" And as we went through the vestry door he added, "You'll think I'm a fool, but to tell you the truth I don't like the idea of being in the church after dark - but I'll explain all about that at tea-time."

We sat in the vicarage drawing-room in front of the roaring fire, and tea was brought in. When he had discharged his duties as host be began to tell me the story of why he had summoned me - hesitantly at first, but his narrative gained in coherence as he went on.

"As you probably know," he began, "I came to this parish last February. My predecessor was a very old man, who was retiring. He'd been vicar for nearly forty years. I spent a week staying with him before I took over, so that he could introduce me to the churchwardens and show me round the parish. He gave me a lot of useful advice, as of course he had known most of the parishioners from infancy. There was one thing that he told me, which struck me as rather odd. It was the question of the vicar's stall.

"I expect you noticed that the vicar's stall was below the altar, by the vestry door. There *is* a corresponding stall on the other side of the aisle - the one hard up against the tomb I showed you. Well, my predecessor told me that there was a tradition that this stall should never be used. Of course I asked him why, but he said that it was an injunction passed onto him by the vicar whom he succeeded nearly forty years before, and that he had quoted *his* predecessor as having passed it on to him. So that must mean that no one for perhaps a century has used that stall. The old man didn't know what the reason was - it was just a local custom that he had respected. I did the same. You don't want to disregard long-standing traditions on taking over a new parish, it upsets people. The stall wasn't used until last night at Evensong, when I sat in it myself.

It's my first winter in the fens, and I find it pretty bleak after Bristol. I'd been bothered yesterday at Matins by the most howling draught under the vestry door. As we went in to Evensong I suddenly had an impulse to sit in the opposite stall. It seemed ridiculous to catch pneumonia out of deference to some absurd local myth. So I crossed the chancel and sat down.

All the choir turned and gaped at me, as though I'd gone out of my mind, and old Mason, the verger, shook his head violently at me, but I stood up at once and announced the first hymn. I felt it was an occasion to assert myself, and we went straight into the service. The choir seemed to get used to my new position, and things proceeded quite normally until the second lesson.

As you probably noticed, we've got no electric light installed yet and the oil-lamps aren't very effective, so it was pretty dark by then. The lesson was read by old Colonel Hartwell from the Hall, and I was looking down into the nave, thinking, I'm afraid, of nothing in particular and feeling rather drowsy. Suddenly I felt a tug at my surplice and simultaneously my knee was gripped by something. In my surprise I shot my hand down. My fingers made contact with other fingers. The icy alabaster hand of the effigy had moved and was clutching at me.

I'm not in a position to know what happened after that. I know I gave a cry and fainted. Old Mason tells me that I stood up and fell forward across the stall with an awful clatter, and of course the service stopped. They carried me across here and put me to bed. I came round an hour later, and the doctor gave me a sleeping draught. I had a tactful word with Mason this morning: he was the first to reach me after I fell. It's quite obvious from what he says that the effigy on the tomb was perfectly normal when he saw it, so it really looks as though I must have imagined the whole thing. But the image was so vivid, and the impression of physical contact with the alabaster hand was so strong, that I can't honestly believe that the whole thing was an hallucination. I've questioned Mason closely on the origin of the tradition that the stall should never be used, but he has no idea why this is so and assures me that no one else has any knowledge of it locally. What do you think about it?"

"Well," I said, "there's one thing we could do, and that is open the tomb."

"I was afraid you'd say that," he answered, "but quite honestly I couldn't face the publicity that such a step would involve. What with Orders from the Bishop and a Home Office Permit one could never keep the thing quiet. I'm such a newcomer, you see, and I've already upset local prejudices by last night's effort. I suppose there is nothing else you can suggest?"

"You move back to your old seat," I said, "and in the meantime give me a few days to do a little research on the occupant of the tomb. I'll take a note of the inscription, and I'll photograph the effigy in the morning. Of course, I can't promise any result, but I can't think of anything better to do."

Nothing else happened on that visit which is relevant to this narrative, and I returned to Town on the following day. Now I was particularly busy at the time, and I knew that it would be several weeks before I had the necessary leisure to work upon the problem myself. I sent my notes therefore to an old friend of mine, a Father Andrews, who I knew had made a special study of the history of the English Carthusians. He was indeed himself of the Order. Three days later he rang me up.

"Could you take me down to Brandon St Giles tomorrow?" he said. "I think I may have solved your problem for you, but I'd rather not say anything more until I've seen the effigy on the spot."

We agreed to meet at Liverpool Street at ten o'clock, and I sent a telegram to Travers, announcing our proposed visit. Father Andrews met me as arranged. I had no difficulty in picking out the stout, short form of the priest upon the crowded platform. Somewhat to my surprise he was accompanied by an elderly man of the artisan class, carrying what appeared to be a tool bag. He was introduced to me as Mr Simson, but no explanation of his presence was given. Travers met us at Norwich, and drove us to the vicarage, where he gave us lunch.

During the meal Father Andrews confined his conversation to generalities, and made no reference to the object of his visit. I found his silence on this theme somewhat exasperating though I knew from long experience that he could never resist a tendency to make something of a mystery of things and to seek after dramatic effect. So I concealed my impatience as well as I could, certainly better than poor Travers did. Simson seemed to be a trifle overawed by his surroundings, and ate in stolid silence.

After lunch we all went across to the church and gathered round the effigy. In obedience to some whispered instructions from the priest, Simson produced from his bag a powerful electric torch. Leaning into the dark alcove, he placed it behind the protruding hand and switched it on. Father Andrews gave a little exclamation of satisfaction. The alabaster of the fingers showed up opaque in front of the bright light, but inside them there showed up quite unmistakably the bones of a real hand, severed at the wrist. Travers and I looked on in silent astonishment.

"There is a joint at the wrist," said the Father, pointing to a barely discernible line on the white surface of the alabaster. "With your permission I will get Mr Simson, who is a skilled stone-mason, to remove the alabaster hand. I can assure you that he can replace it without the effigy suffering the slightest damage."

The mason gruffly confirmed this last statement. With obvious reluctance Travers gave his consent, and a stonecutter's saw was brought out of the tool bag. In a few minutes the hand had been detached. The alabaster below the wrist was only a hollow shell, from out of which Father Andrews drew a withered mummied hand, which he reverently wrapped in a cloth and put into his attaché case. Then, anticipating the protest which was framing itself upon the vicar's lips, he said, "This is a relic which is only of value to my Church. I can guarantee that this hand does not belong to the body of your former vicar buried in the tomb below. There is no question of despoiling his grave. Perhaps while Mr Simson is replacing the hand we could return to the vicarage, and I can explain everything."

The three of us went back to the drawing-room and pulled our chairs up to the fire. Father Andrews beamed at us, rather in the manner of a conjurer who has just performed a highly successful trick.

"The clue to this mystery is to be found in the life of John Foxe, the martyrologist," he began, "and it presents many parallels with the history of that unfortunate man. The Charterhouse in London was dissolved by Henry VIII in 1535, but not without bloodshed. For several of the monk refused to recognise the spiritual supremacy of the King and were executed. John Foxe and apparently John Melcombe, who erected the effigy in your church, were not, however, strong enough to acquire the martyr's crown. They both took the Oath of Supremacy and received livings in the Anglican Church - Foxe at St Mary Magdalen, Queenhithe, and Melcombe in this parish. However, although they conformed outwardly, they both remained steadfast in the Old Faith. Foxe's subsequent history is well known. It came to the ears of the King's Commissioners that he kept secretly upon his altar the left arm of Prior Houghton, the martyred head of the Charterhouse. Foxe himself fled the country and reached Louvain in safety, but two friends of his, one of them Prior Mundy of Bodmin, were indicted at the Guildhall and sentenced to be hanged, drawn and quartered. This savage sentence was, Iam glad to say, remitted by the more merciful government of Protector Somerset.

"John Melcombe was more fortunate. He succeeded to the living here on the death of Walter Hinkman in 1536. He, too, brought with him one of the forbidden relics from the Charterhouse, the hand of one of his colleagues, who had suffered for the Faith. He knew that if the presence of this relic were discovered, it would mean his death, and so, profiting by the example of Foxe, he did not conceal it in the altar, but found a safer and more elaborate way of hiding it. He erected a monument to his predecessor and incorporated the relic inside it. This monument was on purpose placed hard up against the altar, and one can imagine the secret satisfaction that he derived from this - for when his congregation made their obeisance to the altar, they unwittingly paid their devotions also to the hidden relic. His vanity or perhaps his sense of honour made him mark the place of concealment by an enigmatic inscription - for, of course, *sancta manus* in the hexameter on the tomb means *sacred hand.*

"That is the explanation of the presence of the relic," concluded the priest. "But" he added - and his eyes twinkled a little behind his glasses, "what, of course, I can make no pretence to explain is why the relic should have manifested itself in quite so unpleasant a manner to a clergyman of the Anglican Church."

THE TOPLEY
PLACE SALE

"I WISH you'd tell me all about the Topley Place sale,"' I said.

"What do you mean – 'all about it?'" asked my companion.

"Well," I replied, "I heard that something rather odd occurred in connection with it, which wasn't given any publicity at the time."

Ian Maxwell, a member of a well-known firm of art auctioneers, looked at me quizzically across the luncheon table.

"I think I'm being pumped," he said. "I've no idea how much you do know, but if there are stories going round about it, you'd better hear the truth.

"About six months ago a man named Dunton came to see me. I knew him by name. He was a stockbroker, and I'd once had some dealings with his firm. He told me that he'd just inherited Topley Place, being apparently the nephew of old Sir Robert Topley, who'd just died. I knew that Dunton was a rich man, and my first thought was how fortunate it was that the place had got an owner who could afford to spend some money on it. It's a glorious house, but it wants a little doing to it. I don't know if you're familiar with it. It was described in *Country Life* about ten years ago - an entirely unspoilt Jacobean house.

"Well, of course, I congratulated Dunton on his good fortune, but he seemed very lukewarm about it. He said it was a white elephant, inaccessible and inconvenient, that he would never consider living there, and would let it if he could find a tenant. Then he went on to say, 'I believe there's some very good furniture down there, and pictures, too. I want you to send a man down with me when I go there tomorrow for the first time. I never knew the old man very well; in fact, I only inherit by virtue of being the nearest relation.'

"I said that I would be glad to accompany him myself and asked him if he knew Of any pictures of particular interest. His reply will give you a pretty good idea of the sort of man he was.

"'I haven't the faintest idea,' he said, 'but I can tell you this - if there's anything saleable, it's coming straight up to Town. You won't find *me* keeping thousands of pounds' worth of capital locked up on the walls. I've no sympathy with that sort of sentiment. A fellow came to see me the other day about raising some money - said he was hard up, and I know for a fact that he has a couple of Gainsboroughs in his dining-room! If you'll come down to Topley with me tomorrow and pick out anything good, I want it sold this season. It's no use waiting - prices, I understand, are pretty good and that money might be earning five per cent.'

"Well, as you know, selling works of art is my bread and butter, so I ought to have been pleased, but there was something almost disgusting in the man's eagerness to scatter his dead uncle's possessions to the four winds. It wasn't as if he needed the money. However, I naturally agreed, and we arranged to meet at Paddington at ten o'clock on the following day.

"We had an uneventful journey down to Somerset, and arrived at the house at about lunch-time. It was a really charming place, and had obviously been well cared for, but one could see that there hadn't been quite enough money to make it into a showplace. As it was Dunton's first visit, the agent had got all the servants lined up to greet their new master. It was all rather old-fashioned, but personally I like that sort of thing. It was then that I first realised what a complete outsider Dunton was. The occasion obviously demanded a little speech, but he made not the slightest attempt to be civil and even had the consummate bad taste to start a discussion on the question of staff reduction in their presence! The agent sent them off and started to show us round the house. He was a very decent fellow, called Elliot, a man of about fifty, who'd been there for nearly thirty years. Of course, as soon as he realised that Dunton had brought me down to strip the place of its pictures and furniture, he regarded me with considerable hostility, and I can't altogether blame him. Dunton treated him like dirt, and I was there as Dunton's professional adviser. I don't think I've ever had quite such an embarrassing day, and I'm pretty hardened to going round houses.

"Well, there were some very nice things, and I made a list as we went. There was a big panel of Gobelins tapestry, some very fair armour, a good refectory table, two really fine William and Mary inlaid cabinets, and a lot of other very saleable furniture. The pictures, too, were promising - nothing sensational, mostly good English school, a Richard Wilson, two Zoffanies, as well as a delightful Guardi. In the study there were some modern pictures, none of much account except for one magnificent early John portrait, which I realised was of Dunton, painted probably thirty years before. He told me that his uncle had commissioned it in 1910. I was interested to compare my companion's face with the picture, to see how much material success had filled out the features, giving him all air of complacency that was lacking in the painting. But even in his early twenties his mouth had assumed its present hard line. Of course it didn't occur to me that he would want to sell his own portrait, but he asked me what I thought it would fetch. I gave a rough estimate of three or four hundred pounds, and he recalled with considerable glee that his uncle had only paid the artist a hundred guineas in 1910.

"'The best investment he ever made,' he said. 'Send it up with the rest of the stuff.'

"So I added it to my list and we passed on. I was desperately sorry for the agent. He had grown up with the place and was obviously very proud of it, and I could imagine that on hearing of the wealth of the new owner he had been planning all sorts of improvements. But instead of improvements, Dunton seemed intent on denuding the house of all its treasures. However, Elliot didn't say much, but accompanied us from room to room.

"In the small drawing-room we stopped in front of a picture of a naval officer on the wall. Below on a table were laid out what had obviously been his belongings - a great silver-mounted telescope, a gilt dress-sword with a presentation inscription upon it, and a pair of finely engraved pistols. In a case nearby was a suit of naval uniform. Elliot pointed to them and said emphatically, 'Well, anyhow you can't sell these. They're heirlooms and entailed.'

"Dunton rounded on him angrily.

"'Don't try to teach me my business,' he snapped. 'Do you think I don't know the conditions of my inheritance? I'm not a tenant for life, as my uncle was - I'm the absolute owner of this property, and as such I can sell what I choose. And if I ever require your advice on the subject, I'll ask for it.'

"I hastened to interpose, 'I don't really think that they'd fetch very much in the open market,' I said. 'They are the sort of things that are of the greatest family interest, but they' re not really early enough to attract the collector. I doubt if they'd sell for more than a few pounds.'

"Dunton ignored my remarks, and looking coldly at the agent he said, 'Put them down on the list.'

"Of course the man was a sadist. He was just out to show Elliot who was master. If the agent hadn't suggested that they couldn't be sold, Dunton would have taken my advice. As it was, I had no choice but to note them down. They were perfectly readily saleable, but it seemed so unnecessary to take them from where they belonged for the sake of the few pounds that they'd bring in the auction room. The agent turned quite pale with anger. I thought he was going to tell Dunton exactly what he thought of him. However, he controlled himself and merely said, 'You may be right about the legal side of the question. I dare say there's no actual ban on your selling, but if you'll take my advice, you won't do it. Admiral Topley was a quick-tempered man, and I shouldn't like to ignore his instructions, even if he has been dead a hundred years. It was his expressed wish that these relics should be preserved in his house, and I should have thought that you might have respected his request. However, you won't be influenced by my views on the subject. But don't say that I didn't warn you.'

"On saying this he turned abruptly and left us. Dunton seemed more amused than annoyed. The incident typified for him the sentiment that he found so ridiculously unworldly.

"I looked with interest at the portrait. Though obviously not the work of a first-class artist, one could not fail to be struck by the figure depicted. It was full length and showed an officer in the naval uniform of the time of Nelson, and like Nelson lacked an arm. The empty left sleeve was neatly pinned across the breast. The face was of a proud, imperious man, used to giving orders and to being obeyed with alacrity. The nose was aquiline and the check-bones rather high. I have seldom seen a more obviously patrician face. The artist had caught well the weather-beaten, mahogany complexion born of long exposure. I agreed with Elliot that he bad probably been quick-tempered. He looked as though he would be intolerant of any interference with his wishes, and would bitterly resent any affront.

"We passed on, and I found a few more things to send up to the sale. When I went back to Town that night I had every reason to be pleased with myself. But I couldn't get the memory of Dunton's boorishness and Elliot's distress out of my mind. However, it obviously wasn't politic to quarrel with my client, and if we didn't undertake the sale, I was quite sure that he would merely find another auctioneer. And the Topley Place sale was obviously going to be one of the highlights of a fairly commonplace season.

"In due course the stuff was sent up to our rooms, and we set to work on preparing the catalogue. Our picture man was very pleased with his share of the sale and made a big thing of the Guardi. I decided to catalogue the portrait and relics of Admiral Topley myself. I had an irrational desire to do the old man proud and to write him up well in the catalogue. I searched about for information on him and his career. I didn't find much, though. He had never been a great figure in the Navy, becoming a Rear-Admiral only a year before his retirement in 1807. In 1790, I discovered, he had fought a duel and his opponent had died of his wounds, but the affair didn't seem to have affected his career, because he was a Captain commanding a ship of the line at Camperdown under Duncan, where he lost his arm. The silver-gilt sword was given him by the city of Wells, where he lived at that time. He inherited Topley Place in 1604, but didn't settle there until six years later. He lived there until his death in 1831 at the age of eighty-three. I got my leg pulled a good deal for spending so much more time on the old man than could be justified by the price be would fetch - but I didn't care.

"The catalogue was printed and sent out - I expect you got a copy. A week before the sale, the property was put on view in the large gallery. I had the admiral hung in an alcove, with a table in front of him, on which were spread out his pistols, sword, telescope and uniform. I felt quite ashamed when I saw him there with a lot number in the corner of his frame, looking, I thought, more imperious than ever. I'd done my best to interest a few possible purchasers in him, writing to the Maritime Museum at Greenwich and to Wells about his sword, but I couldn't see the whole lot fetching more than about twenty-five pounds. The portrait of Dunton by John, on the other hand, aroused a lot of interest both in the trade and among private collectors, and I don't mind telling you that we had several substantial bids left with us for it.

"Up to now I expect you've found this story pretty straightforward, but just before the sale something very odd indeed occurred. If I hadn't been so intimately concerned in it and if I couldn't vouch for every detail myself, I should have considerable difficulty in believing it. As I expect you know, we employ a night watchman. We often have fifty thousand pounds' worth of stuff in the galleries, and we can't afford to take any risks. Our watchman is a most reliable man, who's been with us for years - an ex-sergeant from the Brigade of Guards. On the morning of the sale, I found him waiting for me in my office, looking extremely worried. He told me that he had been downstairs at about midnight when he thought he heard a report somewhere in the building. He had a good look round but couldn't find anything, and eventually

47

assumed, very naturally, that he had heard a car backfiring outside. But when daylight came he discovered that the John portrait of Dunton had been defaced.

"Of course when I heard this I went quickly up to the gallery to have a look at it. I don't really expect that you'll believe me when I tell you what I found. There was a round hole in the head, and this was blackened round the edges as though it had been made with some firearm at point-blank, range. The wall behind was not marked in any way and, believe it or not, one of the admiral's pistols had been fired. There was no mistake about that. They had been bright and clean, but now the barrel of one or them was fouled.

"My first thought was to ring up Dunton. The picture was insured, of course, but we should have to withdraw it from the sale. When I got through to his house, I received my second shock of the morning. For Dunton had died of heart failure during the night. Apparently it wasn't altogether unexpected - his heart had been giving him trouble for years.

"Of course this may have been purely fortuitous. Some madman *might* have broken into our premises and defaced the portrait: Dunton's death on the same night may have been mere coincidence. But I know and you know that that isn't the true explanation. It was one of those things which are at present outside the range of human experience.

"Naturally the sale had to be postponed, as we had to get the new owner's instructions before proceeding. Dunton was unmarried and his heir was a married sister of his. She and her husband were overjoyed at the possibility of living at Topley, and they wouldn't hear of the sale going on. Everything was returned to the house. I went down there again the other day. The admiral was back in his rightful place, and though I felt that he'd lost us the best sale of the season, I was delighted to see him there; and I don't think that any future owner of Topley Place will be in a hurry to send him up to the sale-room again."

THE TUDOR
CHIMNEY

I AM an indefatigable note-taker. A lifetime of antiquarian studies has led to a most formidable accumulation of material. Shelves of notebooks, cupboards and trunks of papers bear witness to my enthusiasms, and, I like to think, to my industry. Nor can I bear to throw anything away - I have too much of the magpie in me for that. So far I have successfully resisted the efforts of motherly women friends to 'clear out all that rubbish,' and my commonplace-books of what struck me as curious and interesting thirty years ago provide me with occasional reading matter of a particularly delightful nature. I have indeed, one regret. When I was young and ambitious I vowed that 1 would conscientiously index all my entries, a resolution which 1 kept for nearly three months. The task now is too Herculean even to bear thinking about. Luckily I have a memory above the average – particularly for what the more practical of my friends rudely dismiss as 'scraps of useless knowledge; and one of these despised scraps once stood me in very good stead.

When Simon Venn first told me of his project, I supported it enthusiastically - for he is a very rich man. To restore a derelict house to its former glory is no occupation for the possessor of a modest income. Though the initial purchase of such a property may be effected for the proverbial song, the illusion of a bargain is soon shattered by the long face of the inspecting architect and by still longer accounts from the local builder. But considerations of this nature weigh little with a man whose fortune is based upon the secure foundation of a century-old whisky distillery. The finding, however, of a suitable house for renovation proved surprisingly difficult. He told me that he had explored perhaps a score of properties offered by optimistic agents. He had visited 'Tudor houses', not a brick of which could have been laid earlier than the eighteenth century, and a 'Georgian' mansion which could hardly have been designed before the Great Exhibition. He had seen one or two perfect houses in settings hopelessly spoilt by modern developments, and not a few glorious sites with houses unworthy of them. [n fact, Venn had begun to despair of ever being able to dissipate his surplus wealth in this delightful way, and in a fit of pique removed himself to the South of France.

It was in the following May - the year was 1924 - that I next heard from him. He had returned to England, and had happened upon the ideal house for his scheme in Berkshire. The letter was written in an exultant tone that reflected the enthusiasm of the man. Nothing would suffice but that I came down at once to see it. The purchase had been completed and work was already beginning. He would make no attempt to describe the place - no words could do justice to its charms - and much more in the same strain. There followed minute instructions for the drive down. The letter was headed The Old Hall, Didenham, a village which lay, according to my friend's information, in the Downs between Wantage and Lambourn. Such an invitation was much to my liking. I consulted my engagement book, told several white lies over the telephone, and found myself possessed of four clear days. A telegram to Venn, some hasty packing, and my arrangements were complete. By noon I was speeding along the Great West Road, pleasantly deserted on a fine midweek morning. Lunch at Reading delayed me for half an hour, but by half-past two I was on the last lap of my journey.

Lambourn was behind me, and I climbed steadily up the

second-class road on to the Downs; I have always loved these spacious chalk uplands, and Venn had chosen to settle in an area much favoured by ancient man. The prehistory of the neighbourhood was fairly well known to me - the White Horse, Uffington Castle and Wayland's Smithy had been visited and revisited, but I had never before approached this stretch of the Downs from the south side. Some way short of the summit I turned up a side lane, breasted a ridge and before me I saw what I knew must be my destination. I stopped the car and gazed in appreciation at the scene before me. Three hundred yards away was the house, set in a re-entrant of the hill and sheltered on three sides. I could not see the village itself, but the tower of a church just showed itself above some fine beeches to the right.

From the eminence on which I had stopped I looked down upon the Old Hall, a building whose mellow red brick glared in the afternoon sun. I tried to guess its date, and put it down as early sixteenth century, which I subsequently learned was an accurate estimate. It was built upon an 'H' plan, and at each end was a great multiple chimney-stack, displaying those spiral brick chimneys which were so dear to the heart of the Tudor builder. Round one of the stacks scaffolding bad been erected, from which I presumed that Venn had wasted no time in getting to work. What I could see of the grounds was frankly disappointing. To the front a few acres of indifferent parkland, but behind the house I could just perceive the angle of a high wall which gave promise of a sheltered garden to the rear. The general effect of the whole was somewhat dilapidated but by no means derelict.

I restarted the car, and in a couple of minutes I was receiving a smiling greeting from my host's manservant, an old acquaintance of mine and a great chatterbox.

"Well, Dawson," I said, "how do you like your new home?"

"Very nice, sir," he replied, and by the time Mr Venn's finished with it, it should be a regular showplace. But when he tells me what he's going to do, I sometimes doubt if he ever will finish it - in my lifetime- that is."

'Oh, come,' I said, 'surely it's not as bad as all that?'

'Well, sir,' he responded, 'I shall be very surprised if we get the workmen out this side of Christmas. I can't understand what's come over the master. Take the dining-room, for instance - it may be a bit on the small side, but it's cosy like - intimate, if you know what I mean. Well, Mr Venn is not only joining it up with the drawing-room, but, believe it or nor, he's going to take the first floor out so that it goes right up to the roof. I've never heard of such a thing. Think of heating the place, sir, I said…"

He broke off suddenly as my friend appeared and became very busy picking up my bags.

"I heard you, Dawson," said Venn, laughing, and added as the old man went off with my luggage, "Poor old Dawson, I'm afraid he doesn't appreciate the excitement of tracing out exactly where the Great Hall used to be. I'm delighted that you've come. I do hope that you won't be too uncomfortable. We're camping out in the west wing during the alterations, and having our meals in the library." He glanced at his watch. "We've got an hour before tea," he said, "just nice time to give you a general view of the place. I'll show you the plans for restoration after dinner."

It would be unreasonable to inflict upon the reader an account of my tour of the house, especially as it has little bearing upon the events to come. I will, however, admit that Venn's enthusiasm was amply justified. The latent possibilities of the place were enormous. I saw it all - from the little walled sixteenth-century herb garden to the topmost attic in which were visible the hammer-beams that would become once more the roof of the hall when the intervening floors had been cleared away. In his bedroom Venn showed me with pride part of the original hall screen incorporated in some later panelling. The house was bigger than I had realised- there must have been quite fourteen bedrooms and **it** was just on four o'clock by the time we reached the ground floor again.

"There's just one more thing I'd like you to see before tea," said Venn, leading the way into a small room at the east end of the house. It seemed to be the room in which the workmen had made their headquarters, for it was full of buckets, ladders and the usual paraphernalia.

"What do you think of that?" said my host, "isn't it extra · ordinary?"

He was pointing to the fireplace, which appeared to be the oldest and was certainly the finest in the house. Above the great stone Tudor arch was a chimney-piece of carved oak, richly decorated with mythological figures and heraldic devices. The extraordinary aspect of this splendid relic lay in its being bricked up. The whole of the fireplace had been walled across.

"This room was one half of the small parlour of the Tudor house," said Venn, "and I intend to join it up with the housekeeper's room next door and use it as my study. But can you conceive anyone bricking up this magnificent fireplace and substituting *that*?"

With a wave of his hand he indicated an indifferent cast-iron stove on the other side of the room.

"Thank heaven, they didn't destroy it - one of my first jobs is to get it into use again."

"That shouldn't take long," I said, "providing the chimney

itself hasn't been tampered with."

At this moment a workman entered the room and, seeing Venn there, he touched his cap respectfully. Venn nodded and said, "How long would it take you to knock a few bricks out of this?"

He tapped the walled-in area as he spoke. The workman cast a professional eye over it.

"Well, sir," he said, "if it's only one brick thick, I should say about twenty minutes. Would you like me to 'ave a go at it, sir? just in the middle. I won't go near the stonework at the sides in case I damage it. That'll want 'andling careful."

He seized a hammer and chisel, and as we went off the little room resounded with the ring of steel upon mortar. We had nearly finished tea when the parlour maid brought a message that the man working on the chimney would like to have a word with Mr Venn. He entered awkwardly, cap in hand and said, "Beg pardon, sir, I didn't ought to trouble you, but I 'ope I 'aven't done wrong with that chimney. I've knocked an 'ole in them bricks like what you said, but there isn't 'alf a narsty smell coming out of it. I should say 'ooever bricked up that there fireplace 'ad got a reason for it, sir."

"What sort of a smell?" I asked.

"Well, sir," he said, "It's what you might call a bit 'ard to give a name to. It isn't drains - at least I'd be very surprised if it was - but it's just as narsty. It's as if something's burning what didn't ought to burn. Perhaps you gentlemen wouldn't mind stepping along and trying it for yourselves."

We rose and followed him back to the scene of his operations. As we filed into the room the cause of his perturbation became apparent. There was a smell not very strong but none the less insistent; a kind of kitchen smell, but not the sort that any clean, well-ordered kitchen could produce – an infinitely stale reek of burnt fat and offal. The effect was, to say the least, disagreeable. Venn flung the windows open and some of the pungency was lost.

"I think it's just stale air from the chimney," he said. "Just loosen some more bricks and let's see if it's blocked higher up."

It was the work of only a few minutes to enlarge the aperture to a respectable size, and Venn cautiously inserted his head and shoulders.

"I can see the sky," he said, and his voice sounded muffled and thin, as though it were far away. "There's no other blockage," he went on. "I can't see anything that would cause a smell..."'

He gave a sharp exclamation, and withdrew his head sharply, not before a certain amount of dirt had lodged in his hair. From the chimney came the rustle and thud of falling debris.

"Damn those starlings," said Venn ruefully, looking at his head in a wall mirror. "I thought I saw something moving up inside the flue, quite a big bird by the look of it - more like a jackdaw than a starling, though I haven't seen one round the house. I expect there's a nest up there which wants clearing out."

As he spoke something else came fluttering down inside the flue and stuck on the jagged hole in the brickwork. I took the tongs from the stove and pulled it out, but it was only a small bundle of rags, filthy and charred, and with an exclamation of disgust I dropped them back into the grate. I don't think much else happened that day which is relevant to this narrative. After dinner Venn and I spent an interesting couple of hours in the library with his architect's plans, and there was much talk of butteries, solars and minstrels' galleries which I will spare the reader. We went up to bed at about eleven.

At the foot of the stairs Venn said, "It's a funny thing, but I seem to have got that damned smell in my nostrils; I could swear I got a whiff of it then." I sniffed hard but couldn't be certain. "I'll just see if the door of the room is shut," he added; "otherwise the whole house will reek of it." He returned in a few seconds. "It was shut," he said. "I had a look inside and oddly enough I couldn't smell it at all in the room. Oh well, the whole chimney can be cleaned out in a day or two."

He wished me good night, and I retired to my room, where I slept excellently. I am a reasonably early riser, and the following day dawned so bright that there was no inducement to linger in bed. I resolved to take a short walk before breakfast, and was dressed by eight. It was thus that I inadvertently overheard a conversation at the foot of the stairs. I call it a conversation, though it was more in the nature of a monologue, delivered in somewhat petulant tones by the charwoman, a stout lady of about fifty, who bad been pointed out to me on the previous day. The workman with whom I was already acquainted formed the reluctant audience.

"You men are all the same," the charwoman was saying, "eat your 'eads off and expect everyone to run about clearing up after you. I'll be glad to see the last of you; that I will. Mind you, I'm a reasonable woman, but what I say is that there's necessary mess and there's unnecessary mess. I know you can't carry out alterations without breaking the place up, though why it can't be left like it is, I don't know. But when it comes to strewing your nasty burnt rags up and down my nice clean passages that's another thing altogether. And I won't 'ave it. You've got a room, 'aven't you, to make your filthy messes in…"

'Now, look 'ere, Mrs Fisher,' interposed the workman. 'I tell you straight that them rags is nothing to do with me. There was a few old rags from the chimney, but they was left in the grate. Why should you think I want to go strewing them round the house? I got my work to do."

"Well, you go and get on with it," the acid voice of Mrs Fisher broke in, "and if I 'ave any more trouble, I'll go straight to the master. And that goes for the 'ole lot of you. And if I sees the foreman, I'll give 'im a piece of my mind. About as much good as a sick 'eadache, 'e is."

The workman made his escape and I descended the stairs. The aggrieved charwoman was engaged in sweeping a small heap of charred rags into her dustpan, an action which was punctuated by much muttering.

"Good morning," I said. "It's a lovely day."

She agreed reluctantly, and I hastily passed by, in case she should start airing her grievances afresh. I remember wondering idly how it was that the rags, apparently from the chimney, should have found their way into the passage, but the whole thing seemed too trivial to worry about. I took a brisk walk up on to the hillside, and returned to breakfast half an hour later in high spirits. The day passed pleasantly enough. At about ten my host's architect arrived, and the three of us examined in greater detail what I had inspected cursorily on the previous day.

I liked Henson, the architect, a youngish man and a whole-hearted enthusiast for the scheme. Our pleasure was, however, slightly marred by one thing. In different parts of the house we kept getting occasional whiffs of the smell from the unblocked chimney. On two or three occasions the pungent, unmistakable reek came to my nostrils; then it was gone. Henson smelt it, too, and remarked upon it, but all our efforts to pin it down to any particular place was unavailing. The chimney itself, which we examined, was quite free of it, and its source remained elusive. The flue upon inspection proved to be quite clear. There was no trace of birds or a nest - another minor mystery. I don't want you to think that we took all this very seriously at the time. But I am writing in the knowledge or what was to come, and these apparent trivialities then take on a more sombre aspect.

It was on the following morning that we got our first inkling of more sinister matters. After breakfast I took a turn upon the terrace, and then went to join Venn in the library, where it was his habit to read his morning mail. As I opened the library door I noticed his old manservant Dawson was seated in a chair - in itself an unusual occurrence - and was engaged in earnest conversation with his master. I was about to retire again, but Venn called to me.

"Come in," he said, "and listen to this. Dawson says he's seen a ghost!" His tone was light but his face, which he turned to me, was grave and I could sec that he was worried. I knew Venn was genuinely fond of the old man, and he looked pale and shaken as he sat hunched into one of the library armchairs.

"Well, sir, that's how it is," said Dawson. "I couldn't stay another night in this house, not if you were to pay me a million pounds. Not but what I shall be very sorry to leave you, sir, and after all these years, too, and I will say that I could never hope to have a better master. But I'm not as young as I used to be, and another turn like the one I got last night would just about finish me. I didn't sleep a wink, sir, and I don't think I ever should under this roof. All night long I could see that figure standing there at the foot of the stairs, looking at me. It fair gives me the creeps to talk about it now!"

Venn interposed. "What we'd better do is this, Dawson. You

were going to take your holiday, anyway, in a month's time. Were you going to stay with your married sister at Hunstanton again?" Dawson nodded. "Well," my friend continued, "let's send her a prepaid wire and see if she can have you now. There's no hurry about your coming back - you can take an extra month if you like. And by that time we shall have got this place a bit more shipshape. I expect the upheaval of the move has upset you. But I'm certainly not going to accept your notice straightaway. See how you feel in six weeks' time. What do you say about that?"

With apparent reluctance, Dawson allowed himself to be persuaded into accepting these arrangements. The wire was sent, a favourable reply was received, and by midday Dawson and his luggage had left for the station. Before he went, the old man drew me on one side.

"Look after Mr Venn, sir," he said, "if you'll excuse the liberty. I wouldn't like anything to happen to him. And believe me, sir, there's something downright evil loose in this house."

He shook his head sadly, climbed into the car, and was borne away. At lunch I asked Venn what exactly it was that Dawson had seen.

"That's just the stupid part about it," he answered. "He either couldn't or wouldn't give any coherent account of it - all he did was to keep repeating some nonsense about a figure standing and looking at him. He was so upset that I didn't like to press him for any further details. The only thing he did say at all definite was that the appearance was accompanied by a fearful smell, which is of course suggestive. I'm beginning to think that perhaps I was a bit hasty in having that chimney unblocked. I've a good mind to have it boarded up again for the time being."

"Let it wait for another day," I said, "and we may see

something for ourselves. If you just brick up the hole again, you'll never really have any peace of mind here. We've got to try to find out more about it; a ghost isn't the sort of thing one can shut away and keep out of one's mind."

There the matter was left, and by unspoken mutual consent we made no further reference to it during the day. It is with extreme reluctance that I come to the next part of my narrative. I am aware that I cut no very heroic figure in it, though I hope I am old enough not to worry' about that. But I do not even now like to remind myself of the horror and panic that seized me. There are certain human passions that strip from a man the veneer of civilised culture which normally encases him, that turn him into something primitive and elemental. I felt myself spiritually naked when face to face with the apparition that confronted me that night. But I am anticipating.

Venn and I spent the evening together in the library. He had some letters to write, and I was quite content to smoke and examine his books. At about ten-thirty he rose from his bureau and proposed going to bed. I said that I would read for a while longer, but I hoped that he wouldn't wait up for me. He looked a little dubious at this, but I assured biro that I was quite happy to sit up alone. This was not mere bravado. I felt it unlikely at the time that I should actually see anything. Indeed, I became quite absorbed in my book after my friend had left me. I was sitting not far from the door, and the room was lit by a single reading-lamp. I was smoking my pipe, and after about twenty minutes I found it necessary to refill it. It was then that I first realised that the smell, which I was coming to know so well, was pervading the room. At the first whiff of that sickening reek I sat quite still and listened, but I could hear nothing. None the less, the atmosphere of the room had changed in some infinitely subtle way. The gloom outside the range of the single light seemed to have become more intense and to have assumed an oppressive, malignant quality. The mild May evening seemed to have grown colder, for I was conscious of shivering.

As I sat there, holding my breath, I was aware that I was not alone in the room. Something else was present, immediately behind me. How I detected this I do not know, but I was none the less certain of it. With an effort of will power I slowly turned my head, for I was intensely curious. I wish to God now that I had not given way to my curiosity. For what I saw still haunts me. Just on the outer edge of the lamplight a figure was standing - and I hope I never see anything again so monstrous and so repellent. It was a man, but it had the aspect of no living man. Its form was covered with the charred remnants of clothing. The bare legs were horribly thin; they were nothing but burnt skin and blackened bone. But it was the head that made my very blood run cold. It was hairless and scorched, and the face was nothing more than a featureless, seared, leathery mask. It was the face of a man long dead, but the eyes were alive. They glowed behind the mask with a baleful, infernal light that radiated malevolence. In far less time than it takes to write these words I was on the far side of the door and fumbling with the key. The lock was stiff from long disuse, and I found it would not turn. As I struggled with it, something gripped the handle on the far side and pulled. Sick with panic I tugged with one hand and with the other I wrestled with the lock: with a sudden jerk the key turned and I was standing sweating and panting in the dark passage. On the panels of the door I could hear something scraping and scratching. I ran as fast as my legs would carry me up to Venn's room. He was in bed, but jumped up when he saw me.

"Good heavens, man," he said, "what's the matter with you? Sit down."

I looked at myself in the mirror and realised the cause of his consternation. I was white and breathless, and my face was moist with beads of sweat. He poured me out a glass of brandy from his medicine chest, and as I gulped it down I told him what I had seen. His first reaction was to go to the door and lock it, then he seated himself on the bed again.

"You'd better sleep in my room," he said. "There's a spare bed in my dressing-room that we can bring in here. I can find you some pyjamas. I don't suppose you want to pass the night alone, and I certainly don't."

Far into the night we discussed the matter. Venn decided that as the following day was a Sunday and the workmen would not be coming, he would move his belongings to the inn at Lambourn and stay there for a while. The two servants could easily be given a holiday. The work of restoration could continue by daylight for the time being, but no one would sleep in the house. I questioned him closely on what he knew of the history of the place, but he had little to tell me. He had purchased it in a great hurry, and it had been empty for some years previously. He believed that it had changed bands several times in the last fifty years.

"I do remember one thing the agent told me," he said. "It hasn't always been called the Old Hall - originally it had another name. He told me what it was, but I'm damned if I can remember it now." He thought for a few moments. "No," he continued, "it's no good, I've forgotten - I'd know it if I heard it though."

We agreed to follow up this line on the next day, and to enquire after any local traditions concerning the house. It was some time later that I had an inspiration.

"What about the heraldry on the chimney-piece?" I asked. "That ought to tell us who one of the early owners was. As. far as I recollect, there was a coat of three birds' heads - ravens, I think. It may well have been a canting device. Does the name Raven mean anything to you, or perhaps Crow? Or some combination incorporating either of them - Crowby? Crowley?"

"Crowsley!" interjected Venn, "that was it! Crowsley Hall was the original name."

I was silent for a long time. The name of Crowsley had stirred some vague chord in my mind, and I lay pondering where I had heard it before. At last I thought I had it. It must have been nearly twenty years before, when I examined and catalogued a vast mass of manuscript materials relating to the counties of Wiltshire and Berkshire in the genealogical and topographical collections of an early nineteenth-century antiquary, which were still in the possession of his descendants. I was almost certain that embedded somewhere in my voluminous notebooks I had some information relating to the name of Crowsley, and I decided that it was worth a visit to London in the morning to see if I could find it.

I set off early, leaving Venn to arrange for the move to Lambourn, where I promised to join him in the evening. I spent the day delving among my accumulated papers, and cursed myself, not for the first time, for my failure to compile an index. The afternoon was well advanced before I found that my memory had not played me false. I had made extensive notes upon the family of Crowsley, and particularly upon that branch of the family to which Crowsley Hall had belonged. And certain passages which I had transcribed twenty years before seemed to have a considerable bearing upon our present troubles. I returned to Lambourn forthwith, and this is the gist of what I had to tell Venn after supper.

The fortunes of the house of Crowsley were founded, like those of many more famous families, upon lands acquired at the dissolution of the monasteries. A certain Thomas Crowsley was in a peculiarly favourable position at this period, as he was steward to the great Benedictine Abbey of Abingdon, and was thus able to sell to himself several of the Abbey's richest manors, upon exceedingly advantageous terms. Among these he purchased Didenham, with its small manor house, which was largely rebuilt and named Crowsley Hall by its new occupant. Thus it was that almost overnight the steward of comparatively humble origin became a landowner. His elevation to the status of gentleman was not long delayed, as he received a grant of arms in 1547 and chose for his coat the punning device of the three birds' heads (*party per fess or and sable three crows' heads erased counterchanged*). This was embodied in the great oak chimney-piece, as we have seen.

The majority of such parvenu families quickly adapted themselves to their new positions, and in a generation were indistinguishable from the long-established gentry - but this was not the case with the Crowsleys. In modern parlance they did not 'fit in'. They lived in constant friction with their neighbours, with whom they indulged in an orgy of bitter litigation. The Elizabethan records of the Court of Common Pleas leave no doubt upon this point, and their impudent arrogance is attested by a contemporary letter in which the writer refers to the whole family as 'a saucy overweening contumelious brood'. Nor did the passing years seem to improve matters, for by the days of the early Stuarts they had become the most universally detested family in the county. I have tried to sketch this background of intense local unpopularity because it had direct bearing upon the sequel.

In 1640 the head of the family was a certain Julius Crowsley, a bachelor who lived alone at the Hall. He possessed all the unpleasing characteristics of his immediate forebears and his arrogance and insolence were a byword. He was, moreover, unfortunate enough to deliver himself into the hands of his enemies. One day he was out riding beyond the bounds of his estate. A closed gate barred his path and he shouted to a boy standing nearby to open it for him. Whether the boy made some impertinent reply or was merely slow in complying, history does not relate, but the horseman lost his temper. He felled the child with the butt end of his whip and passed on. The boy, who was the son of a much-respected yeoman fanner, sickened and died. The smouldering resentment of the countryside broke into flame, and Julius Crowsley was apprehended by the sheriff's men, and brought to trial. In view of the high feeling that his action had aroused, the prisoner exercised his option to be tried, not at the Reading assizes 'by his country', but in London. Here he managed to produce medical evidence that the boy was already ailing, and in view of the conflicting testimony of the doctors he escaped with a fine. On May 1st, 1640, he returned to his manor in triumph. The county was in an uproar. Two nights later a party of friends of the bereaved family broke into the house, intent on vengeance. What occurred is not recorded. Julius Crowsley disappeared and his body was never found, nor were his assailants ever arrested. A conspiracy of sullen silence hung over the area and the missing man's servants appear to have been terrorised into holding their tongues. It is more than likely that the sheriff was half-hearted in his attempt to find the culprits, particularly as it was not certain whether the man was dead or had merely taken flight. The sheriff, too, would probably have shared the general approval which greeted Crowsley's disappearance, and in any case the Civil War would have turned men's thoughts into other channels.

These were the facts I had gleaned from my notes. It needed little imagination to supply the end of the story. I could picture Julius Crowsley in his house that evening, startled by the sudden arrival of armed men, his surprise turning to panic as he realised their mission. He would have sought about for some hiding place, and some unlucky chance must have led him to climb up into the chimney of the small parlour. Perhaps his presence there was detected or revealed by some treacherous servant, and his merciless pursuers kindled a fire in the hearth. I could picture the man's feelings as the first spirals of smoke eddied round him, and the tongues of flame began to lick around his feet. He would blindly have climbed higher, desperately clawing at the sooty brickwork. The chimney was too narrow at the top to allow the passage of a man's body, but one hopes that he was suffocated by the smoke into merciful unconsciousness before the flames had done their work. So much one could guess. Yet why was the spirit of the tortured man not at rest?

Venn was deeply interested in my narrative. The rest of the story can be told in a few words - how we summoned Henson, the architect, upon the following day, how close examination of the chimney revealed a disused side flue, which with some difficulty was uncovered behind the wainscoting in the room immediately above. The pitiful remains which we unearthed there were given a decent burial in the little churchyard of Didenham. The sombre shadows of mystery and horror were thus dispelled and the old house was at peace once more. The work of restoration is now complete, and I am a frequent visitor. Dawson is in residence again, and is as talkative as ever - except upon one particular subject.

A CHRISTMAS
GAME

The old country doctor who told me these strange events
has died during the late war at the age of about eighty-live. He
was a medical student at the time of the incidents which he
related, so they can be assigned to the late 'seventies of the last
century. I made profuse notes of his narrative, and I give it, as
far as possible, in his own words. I was spending Christmas
with my family in Dorset – my father was a solicitor in
Dorchester, and we lived in a comfortable Victorian house
about three miles south of the town. The party in the house
was a large one. It included my mother and her two
unmarried sisters - my Aunts Emily and Gertrude - my
younger brother Edward, who was then a schoolboy at
Blundell's, and my two small sisters, Bella and Felicity, aged
sixteen and ten respectively. In addition, we had staying with
us our young cousin Giles; and a number of young people in
the neighbourhood were constantly coming to see us, so
everything indicated that we should have a festive Christmas
holiday. I myself, the eldest son, was a medical student in
London, and I arrived home on the afternoon of December the
22nd. Rather to my surprise my father was away when I got
there, for he led a fairly leisurely existence, and normally took
a clear week off for Christmas.

I was told, however, that he had had to go to Exeter on
business and would be returning that night. It was about nine
o'clock when I heard the wheels of our dogcart on the drive
and I ran out to greet my father. I was astonished to sec that he
was not alone; for nothing had been said about his returning
with a guest. However, a tall, elderly man dismounted with
him, very much muffled up, who was introduced to me as Mr

Fenton. My father asked me to take the dogcart round to the yard and to see to the horse, and he passed into the house with the stranger. When I returned, I met my mother in the hall. She seemed to have lost some of her normal placidity.

"Really," she said, "your dear father is the most impulsive man. He met Mr Fenton in Exeter, and apparently he knew him years and years ago. On hearing that he had nowhere to go for Christmas, he asked him to come and stay with us. He is so hospitable, and says that he couldn't bear the thought of anyone spending Christmas alone at an inn. I know that I ought to feel the same, but I had been looking forward so much to having just the family round me, and however nice Mr Fenton may be, he will still be a stranger. However, we must just make the best of it. Giles will have to move into Edward's room..." and she digressed into domestic affairs.

In the drawing-room I was first able to get a proper view of our guest. He was old, I should think sixty-five, but he carried himself well. His face was bronzed and he had a high colour; his nose was aquiline and he had a patrician air about him. His expression was not a kindly one - it was hard, even forbidding in repose, and I could picture him as being given to fits of imperious anger. Altogether I fully shared my mother's regrets that such a stranger should have been introduced into our family circle at the Christmas season. Nevertheless, he greeted me politely and expressed his gratitude that my father had taken pity on his solitary condition, and he said that he hoped his presence would not in any way interfere with our plans. As a matter of fact, he proved a singularly unobtrusive guest, and seemed quite content to withdraw to my father's study with his book and his cigar, or to take long, solitary walks. At meals he took his share of the family small talk and made himself quite a favourite with my aunts.

It was at a meal - dinner on Christmas Eve - that I committed inadvertently what seemed to be a faux pas. Something in our guest's conversation had given me the idea that he had travelled extensively. In some way or other discussion at table had turned itself to the topic of New Zealand, and in order to bring Mr Fenton into the conversation, I asked him if he had ever been there. He replied with the curt monosyllable 'Yes' and at once changed the subject. I caught a warning glance from my father's eye at the top of the table, and he gave an almost imperceptible shake of the head. After dinner he drew me to one side.

"I shouldn't raise the topic of New Zealand with Mr Fenton," he said. "I have done so myself on one occasion and he obviously found it distasteful. I know that he spent some years as a young man in the Colonial service, and I believe now that I remember hearing that some sort of scandal was circulating at the time of his retirement. I never knew the details - it was the merest rumour and nearly thirty years ago now."

"When did you know him before?" I asked.

"As a boy," he replied. "His father owned considerable property in these parts, but he made a number of unwise speculations in railway stocks and died a comparatively poor man. That was no doubt the reason why his son went into the Colonial service. He has really changed very little since I first knew him. I recognised him at once."

Christmas Day passed pleasantly enough. No doubt modern children would have found it intolerably dull, but we were content with simpler pleasures. The whole household went to church in the morning, and after luncheon the young people went for a walk with the dogs. It was not until we'd had our tea that the serious business of the day began. We all went into the drawing-room, where the Christmas tree had been set up; the servants filed in under the watchful eye of Watkins, our old butler, and we all received our presents. I was gratified to get a sovereign neatly wrapped in tissue paper, from Mr Fenton, and my younger brother and two sisters received half a sovereign apiece from the same source. He seemed to be entering into the spirit of the occasion, and was quite genial at dinner, which followed at six. After the meal my smallest sister, Felicity, was sent up to bed, which occasioned a few tears, and the rest of us proceeded to play various games, such as Dumb Crambo and Forfeits, and the evening passed merrily.

At half-past eleven we started to play a game which had become almost a family institution. It was simple in the extreme. The lights were extinguished and a screen was drawn in front of the fire; then my father began to tell us a horrid tale, which gave rise to many delicious shudders. We children knew it almost by heart, but it never lost its appeal. It was my role to assist him in this, by passing round in the darkness certain objects which illustrated the story. I expect our modern psychoanalysts would say that it was harmful to the young, but in those days, thank God, we weren't burdened with that sort of moonshine.

I still recall the plot of my father's tale. It described how a lonely traveller in North America had to pass through a dark, almost impenetrable forest. Night overtook him before he had reached his destination, and he became aware that stealthy footsteps were following him. Suddenly he heard the dreaded sound of the Indian's war-whoop, and he was surrounded by a band of yelling savages who despatched him with their tomahawks. The abandoned wretches proceeded to dismember the corpse - first the scalp was removed. This was my cue to pass round the circle an old strip of a fur rug, which was greeted with much giggling and with exclamations of disgust from my aunts. Then my father described how the tongue of the victim was cut out, and I sent passing from hand to hand a small padded wash-leather bag, which I had carefully damped with glycerine. Finally the unfortunate man's eyes were gouged out, and this was the signal for my pièce de résistance. Two large muscatel grapes had been peeled and I picked them "I'"" hand them to my neighbour.

This was Mr Fenton. He seemed unwilling to receive them, but I found his left hand in the darkness and thrust into it the slimy horrors. To my astonishment he gave an inarticulate half-strangled cry of disgust, and rising from his seat he snatched aside the fire screen and hurled the grapes into the flames. Then he took a step back and slumped into his chair, breathing heavily. An embarrassed silence fell upon the room, broken by my lather's anxious query of "Are you all right, Fenton?" There was no reply. In the flickering firelight I could see my father fumbling with a lamp. As the light came up we could see that our guest was lolling back in his chair with his head drooping at an unnatural angle. He was very pale and his eyes were closed.

I expect you can imagine the confusion that broke out. My sister burst into tears, and one of my aunts started to scream hysterically, until my mother led her from the room. My father sent my cousin Giles post-haste for the doctor, and in the meantime he tried to revive Fenton with brandy. In the midst of all this, I was the only one present who looked into the fire. I suppose I wondered subconsciously why our guest had reacted so strangely to the grapes I had passed him. Anyhow I bent down to look into the grate for them. You won't believe me when I say what I saw. I swear that instead of grapes there was a pair of eyes, sizzling and sputtering in the flames. I know I wasn't mistaken, and I know they were human eyes. I'd seen enough in the dissecting-room to make no error about that. I was dreadfully shocked, but in some curious way I didn't question the evidence of my senses.

I realised that I had come face to face with something outside the scope or my comprehension - something in which all my scientific training would be of no avail. I resolved to keep my discovery to myself - for I could visualise the effect that any disclosure on my part would have upon that overwrought room. So I seized the poker and brought the flaming logs tumbling down, and those dreadful relics were buried from sight.

All this took only a few seconds, and I was quickly helping my father to revive the prostrate man. A cursory examination showed that he was the victim of some sort of stroke – a condition beyond the range of my elementary medical knowledge. I was therefore relieved when Giles returned in a few minutes with the doctor, who was a near neighbour. He seemed to take a grave view of our guest's appearance. Under his direction we carried the unconscious figure up to his bedroom and undressed him, leaving him alone in the doctor's care.

By this time it was very late. The other members of the household had gone quickly off to their beds, and I went to my room, where I sat down for a few minutes to try to collect my thoughts. The house was now almost silent, and I was oppressed by my extraordinary experience. I tried to persuade myself that I'd been the victim of some sort of optical illusion - that the eyes had existed only in my imagination; but I had seen them so distinctly - the pupil, the iris, every detail. They had been dark brown, almost black. The more I thought about it, the more I was appalled and dismayed. The transition from the cheerful atmosphere of the Christmas party had been terrifyingly abrupt. It was as though a curtain had been lifted for a moment, and beyond it I had glimpsed another world, exempted from the laws of Nature. I recalled an old piece of ecclesiastical dogma that I'd heard quoted, "God may work above Nature, but never contrary to Nature." If I had observed a miracle, it had certainly no Divine origin.

My meditations were interrupted by a noise from downstairs, the intermittent scratching and whining of a dog, and I recollected that in the excitement of the evening, no one had put our spaniel, Danny, outside before locking up. I went down and let him out through the door in the drawing-room, which led on to the terrace. Then, as I had a few moments to wait I lit the lamp and seated myself on the sofa. The idea of waiting in that room without a light did not appeal to me. The fire had died to a few glowing embers, and whatever had been put there had been utterly consumed.

The minutes passed and I became impatient. I went to the door and whistled, but Danny did not come. He was normally a most obedient dog, and his behaviour seemed quite unaccountable. Suddenly he began to howl, low at first but increasing in mournful intensity, making an eerie sound that sent shivers down my spine. I realised that he had gone down the drive into the shrubbery and I called him again sharply, but again with no result. Seriously irritated, I went out to find him and after some difficulty I located him in the laurels.

He was still whining and whimpering when I came upon him, and as he paid no attention to my command to follow me back to the house, I stooped and picked him up. I was surprised to find that he was trembling violently, and as soon as he was in my arms he pushed his head inside my jacket and kept it there, while his body twitched and quaked. I turned towards the house and took a few steps up the drive. Then I stopped as though transfixed. I had left the garden door of the drawing-room open, and through it the light was streaming out on to the terrace. Into this ray of light a figure was moving, approaching the open door with faltering steps. It became silhouetted in the doorway, and I was able to see its outlines clearly. It was a fantastic, incredible form to see in the familiar setting of my Dorset home. It was not a white man. I could see the gleam of a golden-brown body and a head covered with glossy black hair. One side of the face was visible and it was heavily tattooed. A short skirt of rush or flax was its sole covering, and its feet were bare. In one hand it held a stick, and I realised that it was blind, for it tapped gently upon the paving- stones and felt its way towards the door. In another moment it had passed into the room and was lost to my view.

I silently changed my position in order to see more, and in doing so I came nearer to the house. The figure came once more into my range of vision, and I saw that it was on its knees before the chair in which our guest had been sitting, and that it was searching feverishly upon the floor, groping blindly round the chair legs with claw-like hands. I was near enough to hear it give a deep sigh of vexation as it found nothing. Then it turned to the remains of the fire and with fascinated horror I watched it plunge its hands into the still glowing embers and pull them out on to the hearth. It scrabbled in the red-hot ashes for a moment or two, then it gave a low cry, almost heart-rending in its bitterness and despair. No soul in limbo could have given vent to a sound more fraught with desolation. As I stood watching, it rose silently to its feet and moved across the room, out of my sight once more.

For some reason I was no longer afraid, just amazed and curious. I take no particular credit for this; I divined in some obscure way that the apparition, or whatever it may have been, was not malevolent to myself. So you need not think that I was exceptionally brave when I tell you that I strode quickly across the terrace and in through the door. The room was deserted; a second's glance told me this, and as I stood there the inner door of the room opened and my father came in. If the strange visitant had left, it could only have done so by the door at which he entered, and he must surely have passed it in the passage.

"Did you see anyone as you came in here?" I asked.

My father frowned and replied sharply, "What are you talking about? Why on earth don't you go to bed? Shut the door and go upstairs at once. It's nearly two o'clock."

I glanced at the fireplace before replying. There were the embers, scattered about the hearth-unshatterable testimony that my eyes had not deceived me. But I didn't say anything to my father about it. I went somewhat in awe of him, as did many sons at that date, and there was no very complete and frank understanding between us. I feared his anger and I feared his ridicule: I knew that any revelation on my part must bring both upon my head. So I stammered out something about having let the dog out, holding out the now quiescent Danny as evidence for my words. Then 1 quickly locked up. My father waited until I'd finished.

"Fenton's pretty bad, I'm afraid," he said; "but the doctor says that there's a chance of recovery. I'm glad I asked him here. I wouldn't like to think of any friend of mine being taken ill staying alone at some inn. I'm sorry that it has spoilt our Christmas, though."

We went up the stairs together, and on the landing my

father wished me good night. As he did so, we heard a confused noise from Fenton's room. The old man must have recovered consciousness, for we could perceive quite distinctly his rather high, querulous tones intermingled with the quieter phrases of the doctor. As we listened the patient's voice became louder and we caught his words.

"Keep him off - keep him away," he was shouting, "for God's sake, don't let him come near me."

Some reassuring remarks of the doctor's followed, but Fenton didn't seem to be pacified.

"Can't you see him?" he cried. "Over there by the window!"

His voice became shriller and he lapsed into some foreign language that l did not understand. The doctor's tones became louder and more authoritative as he said, "Lie down, sir, lie down. I tell you there's nothing there. I assure you that there's no one in the room but you and myself!"

I looked questioningly at my father for direction, but he shook his head and said, "I don't think we'd better go in. There's nothing we can do. Leave it to the doctor."

He was interrupted by another series of cries, culminating in the sound of a struggle, as though Fenton were being forcibly held down upon his bed. Then, quite suddenly, there was utter silence for a period of perhaps two minutes. We waited, straining our ears. Our vigil was broken by the door being opened; the doctor stood upon the threshold, looking pale and tired.

"I'm afraid he's gone," he said simply. Then, as my father stepped forward, he held up his hand and added, "I should not go inside. The poor devil was in the grip of some terrifying hallucination at the end, and he didn't have a very peaceful passage. Its appearance would only upset you. You go off to bed. I'll make all the necessary arrangements."

We obeyed and tiptoed quietly away. When I got to my room I found that I still had Danny in my arms, and very glad I was of his company for the remainder of the night. It must have been quite ten yean later, when I was qualified and in practice at Cheltenham, that I once a man who knew Fenton's name. He was a retired sheep farmer who had spent twenty-five yean in New Zealand, and though he was too young to have known Fenton personally, he knew him by repute. It was from him that I learned some details of the scandal that surrounded Fenton's retirement from the Colonial service. Dark stories of his ruthlessness and brutality as an administrator had for a time been circulating, but finally were had been an incident which the authorities could not ignore. Under Fenton's direction an alleged malefactor had been subjected to torture, in order to wring a confession from him. When other methods had had led, he had been threatened with blinding, and upon his still remaining obdurate, this dire threat had been carried out. A subsequent enquiry load established the native's innocence, but for the sake of British prestige there had been no public denunciation of the public servant, who had so grossly exceeded his powers. Fenton's only punishment was to be sent home. But though his retribution was light at the hands of men, it would seem that finally he was called to account before a different and a higher court.

THE WHITE
SACK

I had no idea that Tony Marchand was in town until I ran into him in Bond Street. He seemed to be at a loose end, and readily accepted my invitation to dinner. During the meal he seemed silent and preoccupied, and T began to regret having asked him. He had normally a fund of amusing gossip and small talk. After dinner, more for the sake of making conversation than for any other reason, I asked him whether he'd made his annual trip to Skye this year.

He said that he had just returned - then he suddenly blurted out, "Look here, you're interested in the supernatural. Do you mind if I tell you of something that happened to me there? I know you won't laugh at me, and I've been wanting to get it off my chest to someone."

Of course I agreed.

"'As you know," he began, "I've always had a passion for mountains. I know nothing about rock climbing, but I love scrambling among high hills. Don't think that I treat mountains with the over-confident foolhardiness of the novice! Far from it I'm fully alive to my limitations; and while mountains exercise strange fascination over me, they also frighten me. And since my recent experience in the Black Cuillin they've frightened me a great deal more.

"Late this September I was spending a fortnight in Skye in the company of a friend. We had pitched our tent in Glen Brittle. Behind us soared up the southern peaks of the great horseshoe-shaped range of the Cuillin. From the glen they presented a fantastic, jagged-shaped skyline, all too often shrouded in mist. My friend was a climber of some ability, but out of deference to my inexperience we had spent the first two days of our visit clambering about among the foothills. On the third morning, however, we set out on n whole day's expedition. Leaving at nine o'clock, we soon traversed the boggy grassland that separated our camp from the hills, and the ground became firm and rocky under our feet. The grass became sparser, and finally disappeared as we climbed the west ridge of Sgurr Dearg. Though this is one of the highest peaks, it is also perhaps the easiest to climb, and two hours' clambering found us at the top. Some of the upper stages provided stretches of stiff scrambling, where the use of hands as well as feet was necessary, and I was glad to relax when the summit was gained. The view out to sea was superb. The islands of Canna, Rhum and Eigg seemed quite close, whilst beyond them to the right we could sec the Outer Hebrides, a low chain in an illimitable vista of ocean. We picked them out one by one on the map. Then moving to the other side of the ridge, we looked down into Loch Coruisk.

"Ever since the days of Sir Walter Scott descriptive writers have exhausted their superlatives on the scene that met our gaze, and I shan't try to compete with them. The grandeur of that mighty semicircular amphitheatre beggars description. The sheer rock walls ran right round to the sea at either end, and three thousand feet below lay the blue-black loch, a land-locked stretch of water unrivalled in its sinister beauty. Two and a half miles across the valley lay the great symmetrical shape of Blaven; on its left were the jagged teeth of Sgurr nan Gillean. In the immediate foreground was the Inaccessible Pinnacle, and below it a thousand feet of sheer cliff.

"My friend and Iwere to part here. He was to spend the day on the ridge, while T was to descend on the far side and go down to the end of Loch Coruisk, where it runs over the falls into the sea at Loch Scavaig. On the previous afternoon I had been most carefully coached in my route. To the north of the peak on which we sat was a gully, well known to my friend and marked on the map as a safe walk for the tyro. My path having been described in the greatest detail, I set off along the ridge and duly found the place for my descent. For a thousand feet it was a straightforward scramble. At only one place did I encounter any difficulty, which a little care soon surmounted. The gully ended abruptly and I found myself at the top of a vast scree slope, stretching downwards for fifteen hundred feet. I always find walking on scree an exhilarating experience. One gets the illusion of cheating the laws of gravity; by rights the whole of the loose surface should begin to slide in an ever-increasing avalanche into the valley below - but in fact, of course, it slides a foot or two and then stops.

"The grinding, scrunching noise of my descent disturbed an eagle on the cliffs above, and I watched it wheel away over the range with slow strokes of its great wings. At the bottom of the scree was a shorter stretch of boulder-strewn hillside, and I soon found myself by the shore of the loch. This proved to be surprisingly difficult going. Great glacial slabs were everywhere, and they needed careful negotiation. I was hot and exhausted when I reached the waterfall. It was one o'clock, and the sun was now high in the sky. I unpacked my satchel and consumed the sandwiches I had brought with me, and as I ate I looked back at the great rock wall that I had surmounted. There was not a sign of life in that great howl in the mountains. I scanned the ridge for some sign of my companion, but I could see nothing - nothing except the purple and grey gabbro cliffs and the dark waters of the loch. Any noise was drowned in the monotonous roar of the waterfall.

"I am not usually affected by solitude, but even in the bright sunlight I was not insensible to the sinister associations of the place. Queer unwelcome fancies began to obtrude themselves upon my imagination. I got the impression that in the dark shadows of those cliffs unseen watchers had me under observation, and I felt that their interest in me was the reverse of benevolent. I craved for company, and again I ran my eye along the mountain tops for some sign of my friend, but he was nowhere to be seen. With an effort of will power I turned my back upon Loch Coruisk and looked out to sea.

"I was surprisingly tired. I had come perhaps six miles, and my muscles were not yet accustomed to the demands of the hills. The sun was very hot, and before setting off on the return journey I lay down to rest on a stone slab. 'I must have slept; for I had a strange dream. It was a familiar nightmare of my childhood, but it must have been quite twenty years since I had last experienced it. I was back in the garden of our Gloucestershire home, peering through the boundary hedge at the old watermill which lay just beyond it. This mill had exercised an unholy fascination over my brother and myself as children, particularly as the miller was a bad-tempered, cross-grained old man, who detested children and never failed to chase us away with threats when we trespassed on his property. Consequently an air of mystery enveloped the place for us, and there was nothing so evil that we did not believe it of the miller. In my dream I scrambled through the hedge, and made my way along the river bank to the open doorway of the building. The mill was working, and I listened enthralled to the continuous rumble and splash of the great water-wheel, which served as an undertone for the clatter and squeaks of the wooden-gear-wheels and the harsher grinding note of the mill-stones.

"I could see my arch enemy, the old miller, bending over his work, with his back towards me, and greatly daring, I tiptoed past him and concealed myself in the store-room at the side of the building. The walls were lined with row upon row of full sacks, and I sat there in almost complete darkness, for the only light came through the door, which was slightly ajar. I must have been there for perhaps ten minutes, when in some mysterious way the miller divined my presence. He wheeled round suddenly and with a low laugh he hobbled across and slammed the door of my hiding-place. J was frightened and wondered what he would do next, but nothing happened. Then the vibrations that shook the whole building decreased in their tempo, and I realised that he was stopping the wheel.

"Gradually the rumbling and the clatter ceased, and was succeeded by comparative silence, broken only by the sound of the millstream. I sat there in the darkness, straining my ears. Suddenly my attention was distracted by a sound I detected in the store-room itself. The great white sacks which lined the walls seemed to be moving, slowly but none the less surely, inwards. I could just see their dim outlines, strangely magnified in the gloom, and above the noise of the stream I could hear the steady scraping of the coarse fabric on the door. Gradually the space in which I stood was contracted in its diameter: it decreased from twenty feet to ten - from ten to five. I tried to cry out, but found that J couldn't. And this, I think, is one of the most distressing features of a nightmare - to strain every nerve to call for help and to find that no sound will come. Then, as always happened in my childhood's dream, just as the circle of great sacks drew so close that they almost touched me, I somehow contrived to break the spell and I awoke.

"I sat up and shivered. Then I looked at my watch and saw that it was nearly six o'clock. The whole aspect of the place had changed. The sun had passed behind the barrier of the mountains and the whole landscape was in shadow. The cliffs which had been a friendly purple and grey were now black and forbidding, and the loch bad assumed the hue of pitch. I lifted my eyes expecting to see the familiar jagged skyline in silhouette, but the sight that met my gaze made me catch my breath. For the peaks were shrouded in mist. Darkness would fall before I could repass that formidable frontier and regain the camp. The mist would probably grow thicker - and every tale of men lost in these hills came into my mind with horrid clarity. I knew, too, with what anxiety my companion would view my non-appearance, and I thought that he might be tempted to wait among those unfamiliar precipices and try to find me. To cross them alone in the misty darkness I felt to be quite beyond my power, and I hastily got out my map.

"I knew that, if I skirted the outer edge of the range on the seaward side, I could get back to Glen Brittle. But it was not quite so simple as that. It was, of course, much longer - probably ten or eleven miles. But between me and the glen lay two great spurs which ran out at right angles from the main range. The first was perhaps two miles in length, and consisted of a series of peaks gradually diminishing in height. To go round it would put at least three miles on to my journey, and I wanted above all things to get back before my friend took serious alarm and roused Glen Brittle Lodge on my behalf. I didn't want the humiliation of search parties going off into the mist to look for me. The map marked a route over the spur to the south of Sgurr nan Eag, and from where I sat I could see the saddle that I must cross. It was not very high, perhaps fifteen hundred feet. At present it was clear of mist, and I set off briskly round the edge of the range, about a hundred feet above the sea. A deep ravine in my path gave me some trouble, but I found a place higher up where I could cross it, and climbed steadily. The marshy heather of the coastal strip gave place to boulders, then the boulders became scree. I had lost sight of the spot where I must cross the ridge, and the scree above me ended in two gullies. I hesitated and took the left-hand one. After a quarter of an hour's hard scrambling it ended in a sheer rock face, and I had no alternative but to retrace my steps.

"The half-hour that I had wasted was an important one for the mist had come down and I could no longer see the skyline. But there was nothing for it but to go on, and I climbed the other gulley as fast as I could. Soon I was surrounded by the damp swirling cloud, which reduced visibility to a few feet and muffled the sound of my footsteps. It was cold, too, and damp. As often as I thought that the summit was reached, I found a fresh stretch of hillside looming out of the mist. At length, however, the ridge was passed without incident, and I started to descend. I was trying to hurry, and this was nearly my undoing, for, missing my footing, I stumbled forward and half fell, half slithered for perhaps thirty feet before I came to rest on some scree. I was considerably shaken, but it was with great relief that I found that I hadn't turned my ankle, or done myself any serious harm. With greater caution I continued my descent, and I came down out of the mist once more. The going was easier; I paused to consider the next stretch of my route, and got out my map again.

"There was still another great spur between me and the camp, but it was very different from the one l had just surmounted. Instead of being a gently diminishing series of peaks with saddles between them, it ran out at right angles to the range and ended in the mighty bastion of Sron na Ciche, perhaps the most awesome mountain precipice in the British

Isles, rising sheer from the floor of the glen to a height of over 2,500 feet. Between the gigantic cliff and Sgurr Alasdair on the main range there were two routes marked on my map as possible crossing-places without recourse to rock climbing, but I could not bring myself to try to find them.

"My experience in the mist had unnerved me, and I decided that, though it would make a considerable detour, I would skirt the spur and not take to the hills again. As I refolded my map, I turned and looked back up the hillside. The mist was slowly dropping down on to me. As I watched I saw its white tentacles writhing their way down through the gullies that I had just traversed. It was like some vast army advancing on me, and leading it were detached white patches and spirals which moved ahead of the main body. I was irresistibly reminded of my dream, and confirmed in my resolution to make my way home at a lower level.

"So I scrambled down the steep mountain-side, and soon found myself in what I thought was the lesser evil - the great peat bog that lies between the mountains and the sea. 'It was not a dangerous bog, if one picked one's way carefully. Frequent changes of direction were necessary to avoid bad patches, and I was soon covered to above the knees with the noisome black mud and slime that J floundered through in my path. I found also that it was almost unbelievably exhausting after the strenuous events of the day. I leaped from tussock to tussock of coarse grass and, as I landed on each, it settled slowly down in to the ooze with a bubbling, squelching sound that drove me on to seek the next tuft. At last I found myself under the great rock walls of Sron na Ciche, and here the ground was firmer. I lay down full length for a few minutes and gathered my strength; the bog had taken more out of me than I thought. Then I skirted the cliffs which soared above my head until they were lost in the mist. By this time it was very nearly dark, as dark in fact as it would ever get in Skye at this time of the year. As I rounded the farthest extremity of the barrier, a sight met my eyes which made me almost shout aloud for joy. Across perhaps three miles of bog I could see the lights in the windows of Glen Brittle Lodge. My goal was in sight.

"I expect you'll think that that was the end of my adventure. I certainly thought so myself at the time. But the rest of my journey was not to be without event. It is not a subject on which I care to dwell, but I will do my best to give you a faithful account of what I saw and what I felt. Explanation I have none, except perhaps that my physical exhaustion was playing tricks with my mind.

"I set out again slowly across the bog. I knew now how tiring my passage would be, and I wanted to husband my strength. I'm afraid that any thought of alleviating my friend's anxiety by an early arrival had long ago disappeared. My sole concern was to arrive at all, early or late. 'I picked my way from tussock to tussock, keeping my eyes fixed on the light ahead. When I had gone about six hundred yards, I turned and looked back. There was no ground mist at all; the clouds still lay at about a thousand feet, but as I looked I saw what I thought was a spiral of mist detach itself from the gloom of the vast black precipice I had left behind me. It drifted forward for a few yards and then Stopped, hanging motionless in the air.

"It struck me as an odd phenomenon - nothing more; perhaps the forerunner of a bank of fog, as yet invisible, which might be coming up from the sea, and I turned my face again towards the light. After a further twenty minutes I rested again and turned my head. My heart missed a beat. The white pillar had moved, it was closer now, perhaps a quarter of a mile away. It seemed roughly oblong in shape and about live feet high. As I looked, it seemed to hesitate and stop too. I took a few steps forward and looked again, and I saw that it was moving in my direction once more. With a sudden access of terror I realised that I was being followed by something-something that could not see me, but could hear me as I squelched and floundered across the bog. I assure you that in that moment all the previous fears and anxieties of the day were as nothing. An icy shiver ran down my spine. I tried to move forward silently. At any other time the idea of a man trying to tiptoe across a bog would have been ludicrous. I assure you that there was no humour in it for me. Of course it was hopeless, and as the water oozed and bubbled round my feet I could see out of the comer of my eye the shape moving steadily on, always seeming to gain a little on me.

"My nerve broke. Never before or since have I given way to such blind panic as possessed me then. I started to run. My exhaustion was forgotten. I stumbled and floundered from turf to turf, and the still night seemed to resound with the awful sucking noise that my feet made and with the hammering of my heart. I no longer tried to pick my route; I ran straight towards the beckoning light of the house in the glen. A small pool lay across my path and before I knew what I was doing I was up to my waist in the ooze and slime of that accursed bog. Somehow I gained the comparatively firm clumps of reed and grass on the other side, and with much kicking and splashing I hauled myself out of the water.

"But this had taken time and one apprehensive look over my shoulder told me that the thing was gaining on me fast. It couldn't have been more than fifty yards away, and I ran as I have never run before. I dimly realised that the worst of the bog was past and that the ground was getting firmer under my feet. I seemed to see another light ahead of me, moving as if to meet me. Suddenly I felt something clutch my ankles, and I went down like a stone. As I fell I gave a great despairing cry, and then everything seemed to be blotted out. I got the impression of being enveloped in some coarse damp fabric; my face was pressed into the moist soft ground, and my nostrils were filled with the reek of rotting vegetation.

"I can remember nothing clearly after that. I have a hazy recollection of being half-dragged and half-carried back to the camp by my friend. The moving light I had seen had been his: he had heard my approach and hurried out to meet me. He laid me out on my bed and poured brandy down my throat. I was prostrate with terror and exhaustion. After a while the latter triumphed, and I fell into a deep sleep. It was sixteen solid hours before I opened my eyes again.

"I was terribly ashamed. In the clear light of the sun I realised what an appalling fool I had made of myself. Iwas abject in my apologies for causing so much anxiety by my fecklessness. I told my friend how I had slept by the waterfall and had decided to come home by the longer route; how I had fallen on the hillside and stumbled across the bog, and finally had given way to weariness and panic. But I couldn't bring myself to speak of the thing that had followed me, and he didn't mention having seen anything. It must have been a figment of my overwrought brain.

"But was it? I cannot believe that I imagined the whole episode. I was tired and worried, but surely that couldn't account for so vivid an apparition? After all, it didn't occur until the end of my journey was in sight and my anxieties on that score were at rest. What do you think about it?"

I was silent for a minute or two. Marchand's narrative had

struck a chord in my memory. Then I rose and walked across to the bookshelves. I took down a recent volume of the publications of the Scottish Folklore Society. In it were printed certain Gaelic legends and stories collected in the last century by that great antiquary, John Francis Campbell of Islay. I found the passage I wanted and handed the open book across to Marchand.

It read:

"The White Sack used to roll itself round men's feet, bringing them down, then, getting on top of them, it used to flatten them out and murder them."

THE
FOUR-POSTER

Habits contracted in youth arc apt to persist for a lifetime. For many years I have run my eye down the deaths column of *The Times* before opening the paper. I am beginning to wish now that I didn't do so. To sec recorded the deaths of one's contemporaries is to feel an old man, while to read of the death of a man like Edward Clarkson, ten yean my junior, made me feel positively senile. He couldn't have been a day more than forty-four, and had not yet really made a name for himself. His subject- British archaeology - was a difficult field in which to shine. About three years ago he had excavated several late Bronze Age urnfields in Dorset, one of them on some land of mine, and the results were published - either in *Archaeology* or *Antiquity*, I forget which. Since then I'd hardly seen him. I felt, however, that I should like to go to his funeral. We hadn't been close personal friends, but an acquaintanceship of nearly twenty years' standing demanded some sort of recognition. Accordingly I took up my paper again to see the time and place of the service, and received my second shock of the morning.

'Funeral at the Parish Church, South Grinly, on Friday at three o'clock.'

South. Grinly! That must surely mean that Clarkson had died at the house of our mutual friend, Richard Manning. South Grinly was a tiny place; he could only have been staying at the Hall. I should certainly have to go to the funeral now. It was less than fifty miles from London, and I could be back in time for dinner. At a quarter to three on Friday a decrepit hired car deposited me at the church. My own car was laid up, and I had come by train to Horsham, where I'd engaged one of the station taxis for the afternoon. South Grinly is a hamlet that lies in the midst of the thick belt of woodland which runs right across the northern part of the Weald, and, though it is only eight miles off the London-Brighton road, it is surprisingly isolated - on weekdays at all events. I passed through the lych-gate and entered a typical Sussex church, with a squat low tower and weathered Horsham-stone roof. There were very few people present, and nearly all were obviously villagers. I recognised the Secretary of a learned society to which Clarkson had belonged, but, apart from him, I seemed to be the only mourner who had come any distance.

The doors at the west end opened punctually at three and the bearers carried the coffin up the aisle. There were only two followers - an elderly bespectacled man and my old friend Richard Manning of the Hall. I thought he looked pale, but he gave me a smile of recognition when he saw me. As he passed my pew he bent down and whispered, "Don't run away afterwards - I particularly want to see you, and would like you to stay the night."

It was a depressing service. Outside it was a day of driving min and high gusts of wind that eddied round the roof of the building, making a low moaning sound in the vaulting. The clergyman officiating was very old, and had a thin quavering voice. That did not do justice to the impressive phrasing of the Burial Service. I glanced round the congregation. What did it amount to? A few inquisitive villagers and two or three people like myself who had attended from a sense of duty. Apparently there was no one present to whom Clarkson's death would mean any feeling of personal loss.

My impression of melancholy was increased at the graveside. The rain had stopped, but the wind was higher and the words of the clergyman were practically inaudible. There was a nasty hitch too. One of the ropes either slipped or broke as the coffin was being lowered, and it fell the last few feet, with an ugly thud as it hit the moist clay. Altogether I was extremely glad when the whole thing was over.

I joined Manning in the churchyard. He introduced me to the other mourner, Clarkson's solicitor, who almost immediately excused himself, saying that he had a train to catch, and left us together.

"I'm awfully glad you came down," said my friend. "I very nearly sent you a wire, and then I thought it really wasn't fair to make you come to such a depressing function. But you must spend the night with me. Have you got any previous engagement?"

"No," I replied, "I'd like to very much. I'd better ring up my man from the Hall, as he's expecting me back at dinner time. You'll have to fix me up with pyjamas and a razor."

He laughed.

"That's settled then," he said. "I think we'll walk back as' it's stopped raining. I've been cooped up in the house all day."

I paid for my taxi, and we set out together down the lane, turning off to the right after a few hundred yards through a pair of rusty wrought-iron gates. We followed the long weed covered drive that ran through the dripping woods. I never came to Grinly Hall without wishing that poor Richard Manning wasn't quite so hard up. It was a property that really would have repaid money spent upon it. As it was, the whole estate had a dilapidated and decaying air, which the falling leaves and wet trees accentuated; I often wondered why Manning had never married. The big house must have been a cheerless place for a middle-aged bachelor. He used to say that he had quite enough to do making both ends meet and keeping a roof over his head, without taking on any further commitments.

"Not much of a turn-out for the funeral!" I said.

"Pathetic-wasn't it?" he replied. "Do you know, the poor devil hadn't got a living relative in the world, and few enough friends, in all conscience. I had no end of a job to find out who his solicitors were."

"He must have died very suddenly," I said. "What was the cause?"

"Heart attack," said Manning. "Or that's what Akenside, our local G.P., diagnosed. Personally I should say" – he stopped, then added – "I don't know quite what I should say, but I think" - he hesitated again, then the words came out with a rush – "I think he was frightened to death in some strange manner, and as it happened under my roof, I mean to find out how!" I looked at him quickly. He seemed deeply moved. He caught my questioning glance and said, "I'll tell you about it later. Let's have some tea first."

We walked on in silence through the weeping woods along the drive that wound its way down the hillside. We passed through a dark alley in the great rhododendron plantation and crossed the narrow lake by the old stone bridge. In the twilight before us I could see silhouetted the tall, square built Queen Anne house. A slight mist was beginning to rise in the valley, and I was glad when we reached the front door, where a pair of spaniels greeted my host with much barking and demonstrations of affection.

Tea was ready for us in the library, and, under the influence of an armchair, a log fire and food, Manning began to thaw and become more communicative.

"Edward Clarkson only arrived here five days ago," he said. "I came across him at my dub recently, and he seemed so much at a loose end that I took pity on him and asked him down for a week. He seemed in quite good health and spirits. Not that he was ever what you would call a convivial person, but at any rate he wasn't noticeably silent or depressed. He seemed genuinely interested in the few excursions I'd planned for him` - we were going over to Cowdray, and I'd arranged for him to he shown over Cowfold monastery. He was quite enthusiastic about seeing a Wealden glass site that I'd found in the woods, and was thinking of excavating - you must have a look at it tomorrow. Altogether I should have said that he was perfectly normal.

"On the following morning - Sunday it would have been he looked a bit washed-out and said that he'd slept very badly. I'd put him in the south spat-e room, next to my own room, and the bed there is really very comfortable. You must have seen it - a big mahogany four-poster. He complained of the high wind in the night, which had made the hangings of the bed rustle and flutter all the time, and had given him the illusion of people whispering in the room. This seemed odd to me, since as far as I knew it had been a particularly still night, but, of course, I didn't say so to him. I suggested that he'd slept badly because it was a strange bed, and possibly, if he wasn't used to a four-poster, the canopy and hangings had given him a shut-in feeling. I advised him to loop them back in future. He seemed a bit out of sorts all day, rather silent and distrait, and he went up to bed early; but I wasn't in any way alarmed about him. At breakfast the next day he seemed very worn and haggard. He said that he'd had another disturbed night. He had looped back the curtains as I had suggested, but the noises had continued. He'd shut the windows to keep out any external draught, but he still had the impression of something moving in the room. When finally he got to sleep, he had the most horrible dreams, which made him glad to wake up again. He could only remember one of them, which he told me. It was an odd sort of nightmare and pretty grisly."

"Tell me about it," I said. "It may have some bearing on what happened to him."

"Well, he dreamed he was watching a scene in a churchyard," continued Manning, "a small churchyard in a town. It was at night, but there was a half moon and he could see the black shapes of the houses round it. Everything was quite still, and yet he knew that he was waiting for something to happen. Suddenly the clock in the tower struck three with a deep booming sound that seemed to vibrate inside his head, and as though this were a signal the gate of the churchyard opened slowly and three figures crept cautiously inside.

"They were dressed in long dark cloaks and hoods which kept their faces in shadow. One carried a bar of iron and another a dark lantern. They tiptoed across between the tombs until they came to a mausoleum with a great stone slab as its top. One of them inserted the bar into a crack in the stonework, and they all levered until it shifted to one side, leaving a cavity about a yard square at one end. This made a certain amount of noise, and for a few minutes they crouched down among the tombstones, hut nothing happened. Then they seemed to have a discussion, almost an argument, as to who should climb down the aperture into the vault. Finally the two men with the bar and the lantern got up on top of the monument and lowered themselves slowly out of sight inside it. The third man crouched in the shadow at its base. From below came the sound of muffled hammering, then a crack as of splitting wood. The man outside the vault stood up and peered into the hole, and a whispered conversation took place. Then he leaned down and took in his hands the end of a long shrouded shape that was passed up to him. With some

97

difficulty he hauled it up and laid it down at the foot of the monument. The two other men emerged, and the stone slab was levered back into place.

"At this moment there was a dramatic interruption. Four more figures appeared suddenly; two ran out from behind tombs and two leaped over the churchyard wall. They ran to converge on the party at the mausoleum, and there was confused shouting and the report of a pistol shot. The man with the lantern dropped on to the stone-flagged path, but the other two took to their heels, and by dodging to and fro amongst the graves eluded their captors and threw themselves over the wall, closely followed by all four of their pursuers. Clarkson heard the sound of the chase dying away in the distance, then there was absolute silence. He went across to examine the man who had been shot, but a glance told him that he was dead.

"The ball had entered his temple. Something then forced him to examine the shrouded figure on the ground. He knew perfectly well what it was, and was filled with abhorrence, but the impulse was irresistible. He simply wasn't his own agent in the matter. He went down on one knee and bent over it. As he did so, it seemed to stretch itself - the folds of the shroud were suddenly parted, and a pair of yellow desiccated arms came up and gripped him behind the neck, forcing his face down to meet its own. His disgust and horror were so great that he almost fainted with revulsion, and, indeed, if he hadn't woken up he said that he would have lost his reason. He at once lit the lamp, and was successful in preventing himself from going to sleep again that night. But he looked really dreadful in the morning, hollow eyed and pale. I was deeply concerned about him."

"What a perfectly beastly dream!" I said. "It's quite clear

that he was watching some body-snatching enterprise that failed, but I wonder what directed his mind into that channel. Had he been reading anything about such a case?"

"I asked him that," replied Manning, "but he hadn't any sort of suggestion to make. He'd never had such a dream before in his life, and as far as he knew hadn't read or thought about such a thing for years. He was pretty jumpy all day, but I tried not to leave him alone too much and kept him occupied as well as I could. The weather was wretched, but he found something to interest him in the library here. At dinner I suggested that he should come and sleep in my room, but he wouldn't do that - I expect because he felt it would be a sign of weakness. However, he agreed to have a lamp alight in his room all night, and when he went up to bed I took it in and saw that he was properly settled. I looped back the bed curtains and fixed the window wedges, as they're apt to rattle, and I told him that if he wanted company in the night, all he need do was to rap on the wall, and I'd come in. He seemed very tired and likely to go straight off to sleep, so lien him and went to bed myself.

"It was just after one when I was woken up by a cry from the next room. It wasn't a loud noise - in fact, it had a muffled, smothered tone as though someone had cried out with his head under the bedclothes. I listened hard to hear if it would be repeated, and I caught a sound as though the occupant of the bed next door were kicking and plunging, or possibly even struggling with something.

"I jumped up and running to Clarkson's door, I flung it open. The light inside had been extinguished and the darkness was intense. The noise I had heard had ceased, but my can could just perceive a son rustling of fabrics. I groped for the lamp and the matches; gradually the room became illuminated. At first I thought that nothing was wrong. Clarkson lay still on his back, and I noticed that the bed curtains had been unlooped and were swinging slightly. It was when I caught sight of his face that I feared the worst. It was ashen, the eyes stared fixedly into space, and on the features was an expression that I never want to see again. The hands were gripping me edge of the blanket, gripping it so hard that they were white and bloodless. I seized his wrist and felt for the pulse; but it had ceased beating. There's not really much else to tell you. I got on to the telephone straight away and summoned the doctor. All he could say was that he'd had a heart attack."

"What gave him a heart attack? That's the question." I said.

Manning was silent.

"You saw nothing else in the room?" I asked.

"I didn't see anything," replied Manning, "but as I stood there groping for me lamp I brushed against something, or I thought I did. It was some soft fabric like wool, but it seemed cold and damp. When I'd lit the lamp I couldn't see anything of the sort. I suppose it was just imagination."

"I'd like to have a good look at that bed of yours," I said. "It's curious that he only experienced these manifestations, or whatever they were, at night time."

"You can see the bed any time you like," said Manning, "but I don't think that line will take you very far. It's been in this house since the eighteenth century, and I slept in it myself for over ten yean as a boy. Surely if there had been anything odd about it, I should have noticed it?"

"One would certainly imagine so," I replied. "I suppose you don't know anything about its origin?"

"As a matter of fact, I do," replied my host. "A few years ago I passed a winter working through a mass of old family papers and account books, and I turned up the original bills for several of the pieces of furniture in the house, the bed being one of them. I think I can lay my hands on it now."

He walked across to a bureau and, opening a drawer, he pulled out a bundle of papers tied up with tape. "Ah, here it is," he said, and passed one of them over to me. I read it with interest.

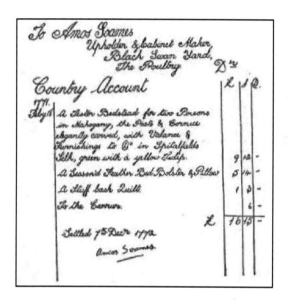

"What a very nice thing to have!" I said.

"It's not at all a bad bed," said Manning, "come upstairs and look at it now, if you like."

We went up to the bedroom. It was a nice bed - nothing really outstanding, of course, but it had an air of good craftsmanship, so often lacking nowadays in all but extremely expensive furniture. The four posts were well turned and tapered gracefully. The tester or canopy had a wooden moulded cornice, decorated with a carved acanthus-leaf pattern. The curtains and hangings were of a faded yellowy green silk, embroidered with a repeated tulip motif.

"These look as though they're the original curtains," I said. "They're wonderfully well preserved."

"It's quite likely that they are," said Manning. "In my father's time it didn't have any hangings at all, but a few years ago the housekeeper produced these from an old press, and as they fitted the bed I put them up. The finding of the bill, of course, confirms the fact that they belong to it."

I lifted the bottom of the curtain nearest to me.

"They're tremendously heavy,' I said, 'There must be a mass of material in them."

The fabric I held in my hand seemed to have three distinct thicknesses - an outer one of the green flowered silk and a lining of black silk. Between the two I could feel an inner thickness of another texture. I examined the lower hem closely and found a frayed section. Here it was possible to see that the inner lining was of wool, rather closely woven and grey in colour. I dropped the curtain and continued my examination, but could discover nothing that gave the faintest hint of the cause of poor Clarkson's strange affliction. We both agreed that the mystery would remain insoluble, and I remember citing the case of the fate of the party who excavated Tutankhamen's tomb and suggesting that possibly Clarkson, who must have opened scores of graves in his time, had inadvertently disturbed the rest of something that it would have been better to have left quiescent. However, this was the merest speculation, and I fully expected that no further light would ever be thrown upon the death of our friend.

Here, however, I was wrong; for there was to be a sequel to these events. Nearly a year later I received a letter from Manning, portions of which I will quote;

"I know you will be interested to hear that some new facts have come to light, which must, I think, be connected with

Clarkson's death. I had the idea of sending a copy of the bill for the bed to ----- of the Victoria and Albert Museum, who knows as much as any man about the cabinet-makers of the eighteenth century, and asking for any information he could give me about Amos Soames. He sent me several pages of notes on his career and on extant furniture known to have been made by him. Of particular interest, however, were some extracts that he had made from a printed account of a trial of 1791. The two defendants, of whom Soames was one, were charged with body-snatching and had been taken red handed in one of the City churchyards. Both were convicted and subsequently hanged. The pamphlet specifically states that apart from his share of the proceeds from the sale of the bodies to surgeons, Soames received, as a special perquisite, the shrouds and coffin fittings, which he employed in the practice of his legitimate trade of cabinet-maker and upholsterer.

"On reading this, I went and re-examined the bed curtains, and went so far as to unpick one of them. My suspicions were confirmed. The grey woollen inner lining had every appearance of former use, and I don't mind betting that it had once been a shroud. Needless to say, I destroyed all the hangings after this grisly discovery, and the bed has been relegated to an attic. I can only assume that the hangings had some baneful influence latent in them. Poor Clarkson, who must have excavated a great many burials, would perhaps have been peculiarly susceptible to it. For, in a sense, I suppose, the archaeologist could be described as a latter-day resurrection man."

THE NEGRO'S
HEAD

THE eighteenth century presents the most extraordinary blend of enlightenment and barbarism. The much-vaunted Age of Reason is but a veneer of culture overlaid upon the credulities and cruelties of a darker period. In places the veneer is very thin and through it the observer can still see at work the sinister forces of ignorance and superstition. It was my fate - I will not say good fortune - to discover the secret of a crime which defied solution in 1759. Not that I wish to blacken the memory of the Coroner, the worthy Dr Pettigrew. I hit upon evidence that was unavailable to him, which was, indeed, non-existent when he held his inquest. Nor can I claim much credit for my discoveries, which were made more or less by accident over a number of years. Yet they piece together into a story of such singularity and such barbarity that I wish to set it down.

Nearly ten yean ago I purchased a drawing by that mysterious and solitary figure, Giles Hussey. I doubt whether a man who is not a student of the art of the eighteenth century will recall even his name. Cried up by Barry as a neglected genius, he is now remembered - if at all - by a series of studies that he made of antique gems. But my drawing was not from the antique. It was a striking study in pen-and-wash of a Negro's head with closed eyes. On the broad brow was depicted a cross, extending horizontally across the temples and vertically from the bridge of the nose to the hair, giving the man the appearance of some fantastic witch-doctor. The arms of the cross were broad and were composed of a continuous floral pattern - somewhat stylised formal flowers, interspersed with ivy leaves. In the drawing it had the appearance of having been painted on the skin or perhaps tattooed. At the foot of the drawing was the artist's neat signature and the words, 'The Negroes Head, taken at the Inquest October 22nd, 1759.' The dealer who sold me the drawing could give no clue to the previous history; it had been bought by him with a large collection of other drawings at the sale of the stock of another dealer, deceased.

I was intrigued. Apart from a natural dislike of having something in my collection that I could not explain, I have always had a morbid interest in sudden and mysterious death. And so I pursued two lines of enquiry. First I sent the drawing to a friend who is an ethnologist specialising in the races of Africa.

I will quote three sentences from his reply;

"There is little doubt that the native depicted originated from the West Coast - his modern counterpart is to be found in Nigeria today… I have never seen any native decoration of the type depicted on the man's brow. Surely the flower and ivy motif is an essentially European one?"

Secondly I tried to trace the inquest. Now this, as you will realise, was not an easy task - I did not know the place of death nor the man's name. I did, however, know the exact date, and I spent a laborious day at the British Museum consulting contemporary newspapers. I was disappointed. The glorious feat of British arms at Quebec and the sad intelligence of the death of General Wolfe overshadowed less important events. It was, no doubt, for this reason that the affair did not achieve considerable notoriety at the time. It should have been as famous as the Cock Lane Ghost. From the point of view of tracing the record of an inquest, 1759 is an unfortunate year. About this dale the practice ceased of depositing the Coroners' Inquisitions centrally in London, and they were filed with the Clerks of the Peace of the several counties. The county systems of keeping their records were at first somewhat haphazard and there are consequently some tantalising gaps in the series. Here however, I was in luck. At the Public Record Office among the Records of the Court of the King's Bench is a bundle of Coroners' Inquisitions covering the dates 1748 to 1767, and here I tracked down my quarry. From the account of the proceedings I noted down the following information: At four o'clock on the afternoon of October 20th, 1759, John Kimble, a fowler, discovered the body of a Negro on the mud flats at Swanscombe Marshes, on the Kent bank of the Thames. The receding tide had left it caught fast on a fence which projected into the water. With the help of a shepherd, Kimble hauled it on to dry land. That night he reopened his discovery to the local Justice. The body was removed to Rochester, where the coroner, Dr William Pettigrew, held his inquest on the morning of October 22nd in an upper room at the King's Head. No one came forward to identify the body, which was of a man of about twenty years of age, wearing a suit of coarse broadcloth. The pockets were empty.

The coroner, summing up, pointed out that there was the greatest likelihood that the deceased was employed as a servant upon some ship, and that he had fallen overboard into the Thames. A juryman drew attention to the sign on the man's forehead, and the coroner made some remarks on 'heathenish and idolatrous practices'. The verdict was returned of 'Found Drowned', and the body buried the following day in the churchyard at the expense of the parish.

So, I thought, ended my investigations. I had learned a little, but the main mystery of who the man was and how he met his death remained unsolved. I felt that it was probable that it was some foreign ship from which the Negro had fallen, and that the chances of adding anything to my knowledge of the subject were remote indeed. Had it not been for an extraordinary coincidence, this would have been the case.

I am a collector of catholic tastes. The highly specialised collection seems to me to be an arid thing, more suitable to the museum than to the library of the amateur. My purchases range over drawings, manuscripts, books, prints., Bronze-Age antiquities, repeating watches and astrolabes; these are main headings only. I find it difficult to resist the rare and curious in almost any sphere of the antique.

Perhaps one of my more peculiar enthusiasms is the collecting of early bookbinders' tools. Bindings themselves have long been a love of mine, and what would be more natural than to supplement the books by purchasing the presses, stamps, fillets and rolls of what I fear, a dying craft? Such things are hard to find; and, though one or two of the older London binders have preserved in situ much of the equipment of their ancestors, it is rarely that they come on to the market. Over a number of years, however, I have amassed a small collection of them - ranging from a German roll of the mid sixteenth century to three delicate stamps of Roger Payne's at the end of the eighteenth. A friendly dealer seeks them out for me, and I was glad to hear about a year ago that he had one at his shop, awaiting my inspection. It proved to be a heavy, elaborate roll, of the usual mounted wheel type, such as the eighteenth-century binder employed to produce a broad gilt border on a morocco-leather cover. I ran it idly across a piece of blotting-paper and inspected the result.

It produced a formal pattern of flowers and ivy leaves that looked vaguely familiar. The price was reasonable, and I bought it. It was not until I got it home that I remembered where I had seen the design before. I hastened to get out my Hussey drawing, and down to the smallest details the pattern on the Cross on the Negro's head corresponded with that produced by the roll. I could only conclude that he had been branded with the very implement in my hand. I examined it closely, and on the brass shaft was engraved in a neat copperplate script – 'Jackson, Binder, Cripplegate.'

Here was a clue indeed. I will not weary my readers with an account of my researches in the parish registers of St Giles, Cripplegate, the parish rate books, and the archives of the Worshipful Company of Bookbinders. In the last came to light the manuscript from which I have been able to reconstruct the strange events of 1759. I should like here to express my indebtedness to the Master and Wardens or the Company for permission to quote from records in their possession.

The manuscript in question is a calf-bound volume containing some thirty pages of writing in the hand of Jonathan Shrine, who was admitted to the Company of Bookbinders in 1762 and who died in 1780. The diction is a little archaic for the date, and points to a man of limited education, whose prose style is obviously founded upon his reading of the Bible. I have made a few corrections in the spelling. The Account was written a few months before his death and begins abruptly;

"Now that I am sinking into a Decline I must prepare myself for the hut and awful Journey, and for my Soul's Peace I must set down a Concise Account of a lamentable and ever to be regretted event. For it is not meet that I should carry so weighty a Secret with me to the Tomb; but that I should leave a Monument for Posterity so that perchance those that come after may profit by the Tale of how I, blinded by Superstition and led astray by the Folly and Wickedness of Another, did have a part in the Bloody Murder of a Fellow Creature, though he was but a Heathen Savage. May the Lord in His Infinite Compassion and Mercy forgive a Miserable Sinner the Excesses of his Headstrong Youth."

The narrative that follows is too long to quote in full and I shall tell the story as I extracted it and only quote verbatim in certain instances.

In 1759 Jonathan Shrine was apprenticed to Thomas Jackson, Bookbinder, who had his house and his business in Fore Street, Cripplegate, a few doors from the birthplace of Daniel Defoe. Jackson died in 1767, a respectable citizen, twice Master of the Bookbinders' Company, and on his death left a sum of money to be distributed among the poor of the parish. In 1759 his household consisted of himself, his wife, his daughter Rachel, a girl of twelve, Jonathan Shrine, the lint apprentice, and a second apprentice by the name of Enoch Bond. There were also two women servants. Jackson seems to have been a considerate employer, and life at the Fore Street house pleasant enough. There is painted a picture of the activity in a binder's shop of the period, with some notes of contemporary processes and trade gossip, which, though of considerable interest, must not detain us here. Shrine was a Londoner born, but Bond came from Plymouth, and the two apprentices do not appear to have had very much in common. Shrine dismisses the latter as:

'An idle prattling Fellow, much given to Country Talk of Jack o' Lanthorn, Hob Goblins and Apparitions.'

Both men, however, were united in their love of the daughter of the house, who appeared to have been a lively, affectionate child, in and out of the apprentices' workshop an day. On October 1st, 1759, Thomas Jackson received into his household a Negro slave, Solomon Marsh by name. Shrine suggests in his narrative that he was taken in part payment of a debt owed to Jackson by his brother, a Liverpool ship-owner - and this is likely enough. He approved of the new arrival;

"A Sober, Industrious Young Man of middling height, well versed in the Preparation of all kinds of Meat and Drink."

Enoch Bond, on the other hand, had an unconquerable aversion to Negroes. His youth at Plymouth had been spent in the company of many seamen who had passed their days on the slave trade, and Bond's credulous mind was filled with stories of the Ivory Coast picked up round the quays and yards of his native town.

"He would say that in every Negro a Devil lurked, that be held all such Savage Wretches in Abhorrence for their inhumane custom of devouring and eating one another up, that the King of Darkness himself could not equal them in Cruelty and Lust. He believed that even in Captivity they still continued in the Practice of their Bloody and Barbarous Rites, not to mention Witchcrafts and Sorceries, that it was an evil day that his Master was mad enough to take one such Monster into his house, for surely Disaster must follow."

Unhappily this gloomy prophecy was fulfilled; for within a week of the slave's arrival, the girl Rachel fell from a second-floor window and was killed. The distress of the two apprentices who loved her dearly was almost equal to that of the afflicted parents. Enoch Bond was convinced that the devil lurked in the body of the Negro and never tired of expounding this view to Shrine, who was finally persuaded to share his belief.

"I in my youthful Folly and Intemperance did listen to him and did begin to believe that in very Fact some Fiend lying hid in the Body of the Negro had compassed our sweet Rachel's Death. Bond was for ever crying vengeance, for, he said, if this

Crime should go unatoned, no man can tell who shall next be taken."

And so the two apprentices plotted together how some fresh blow of fate could be warded off. And they hit upon the scheme of exorcising the devil within the slave. Bond, needless to say, was the originator of the plan and worked out all the details. Fortunately for the conspirators, on October 12th, a few days after their daughter's funeral, Thomas Jackson and his wife went to spend three days with the latter's sister at Islington. The two servants were given a holiday, and the slave was left alone in the house with the two young men. I will quote in full the last page or two from the manuscript.

"And when all was made ready Bond called in a loud Voice, Solomon, Solomon; and when he came in at the door he felled him with a great oak staff, striking him a terrible Blow on the back of the neck. This he did by Stealth, waiting in hiding behind the Door. And the Negro lay on his back, breathing heavily and he was at our Mercy. Then Bond, seizing a Binder's Roll from the Fire cried out in our Lord's Words (May God forgive him), "Thou Unclean Spirit, come thou out of him." And he branded a great cross on the Forehead of the man. And he shuddered fearfully and gave a hollow Groan and I could see the White of his Eyes as he rolled them. But on a sudden he became limp and still and the Pain went from him. And he seemed at Peace. His Breathing ceased and when I felt his heart it beat no more. And I was in sore Distress for at that moment the lord revealed to me that he had been no Devil but that we had brought about the Death of an Innocent Man. Already I had a vision of myself at Tyburn with the Hangman's Noose about my Neck. My companion likewise appeared overcome by the consequences of his rash Deed. And so we sat there half sick with Horror and with the Stench of the singed Flesh. Then I prepared a Plan whereby we could escape from the Hangman. First we took all the poor possessions of the Murdered Wretch which might allow him to be traced, and these I buried. Late that night we took the Body in a Cart and avoiding the Watch we made our way to the River's bank. Many times we thought that we should be apprehended, but by good Fortune we reached the River behind the Vintners' Hall and from the stairs there we committed our Victim to the Water and he was borne out of our sight. And when our Master returned we told him that Solomon had run away. He caused some new Enquiries to be made, but in his Grief at his Daughter's untimely end did not raise any great Hue and Cry. For many weeks we scanned the Public Prints with Fear in our Hearts but no Report of the Finding of the Body was ever put abroad in them. And although Enoch Bond escaped the justice of Man he could not escape the vengeance of Divine Providence that protects even the Meanest of Mortals, that does note even the Death of a Sparrow as the Scriptures tell us. For not a week later we had occasion to go upon an Errand by Water and off the Globe Stain our Waterman did heedlessly set his Skiff in the Wake of a great Indiaman and we were overturned. And the Waterman and I clung to the Upturned boat but Bond, who had swum since his youth, gave a great Cry - Solomon, Solomon, and sunk as though a Millstone bad been hanged about his Neck. And whereas the Generality of men rise three times from the Stream's Bed he rose not at all, nor was his Body ever recovered. And from that Day to this I have never set foot in a Boat lest the Vengeance of the Lord should overtake me also. But I have been spared these twenty years, and now that my End is near I do set down this True Account as a Warning to Youth and for the Good of my Immortal Soul.

"Jonathan Shrine. The 17th day of January, 1780"

When I was last in Rochester I tried to discover the whereabouts of Solomon Marsh's grave, but there is no record of it. I felt that I would like to have paid some small tribute to the memory of a savage who was so grievously wronged at the hands of one of my own countrymen. And with the story of his fate in my mind, I am apt to smile a little ruefully when I hear people speak glibly of the Age of Reason.

THE TREGANNET
BOOK OF HOURS

Many artists have tried to depict the supernatural, usually with a singular lack of success. To me the average picture of the ghost in Hamlet in an illustrated Shakespeare suggests nothing more sinister than a game of charades. A few artists do seem to envisage what a man *ought* to feel when he sees a ghost and try to produce that effect on the spectator. Fuseli achieved some slight measure of success; Goya a great deal. The latter, I feel, really had experienced what he depicts. But on the whole ghosts seem carefully to avoid appearing to anyone capable of putting down on paper exactly what he saw. Which makes me all the more sorry that I did not see be fore its destruction what must have been a very remarkable miniature.

Some time ago I bought at a sale on illuminated manuscript - a Book of Hours. It was of the normal late-medieval pattern - a Calendar of Saints, the devotions for the Canonical Hours, and the order of service for baptisms and Burials. The illustrations were the usual complement of twelve miniatures containing scenes from the lire of Christ. The book was written on fine white vellum and the binding was of old red velvet.

Such was the fifteenth-century manuscript that I bought in a moment of reckless extravagance. And lest it should be supposed that I am a collector of the calibre of Pierpont Morgan or Richard Heber, I hasten to add that it was a very modest Book of Hours indeed, such as would have found no shelf-room in the cabinet of a Duc de Berri. Its decoration and miniatures were of a kind that experts disdainfully dismiss as 'shop work'. It was, in fact, produced in Flanders for the English market about 1480, and though competently written and illuminated, it was no great work of art. Nevertheless, I was inordinately proud of it, for it was the only illuminated manuscript that I owned.

A friend of mine dined with me soon after. He works in the Department of Manuscripts at the British Museum. After dinner I said to him with feigned nonchalance, "By the way, I picked up a nice little Book of Hours the other day," and handed him my treasure.

He examined it with the greatest care leaf by leaf and then said, "What a pity that the miniature illustrating the Burial Service is a modern copy."

To say that I was mortified is putting it mildly. I looked at the miniature in question carefully. Like nineteen out of twenty miniatures illustrating the Burial Service, it depicted the Raising of Lazarus. My friend was, of course, correct. Although the style was extremely close to that of the other miniatures, minute inspection with a glass revealed the fact that it was of modern workmanship, and that it had been inserted by pasting it to the stub of a leaf which had been cut out. My friend tried to salve my wounded vanity.

"It's an extraordinarily good copy," he said. "I think there's only one man alive today who can produce that sort of work. I wouldn't mind betting that an old man named Clarkson painted that miniature. If I hadn't already seen some of his work at the Museum, it would have completely taken me in."

"Is he a forger?" I asked.

"He'd be most offended if you called him that," he replied. "He is a most accomplished illuminator, and his main work is Rolls of Honour, Addresses and the like. But he will also undertake commissions for the reproduction of medieval manuscripts, and a very good job he makes of them!"

I agreed ruefully. After my friend had gone I re-examined

the book, but could discover no other peculiarities except for one small point. A shield on the lint leaf had apparently once contained a coat-of-arms, but the arms emblazoned there had been carefully erased; and by the whiteness of the vellum below I thought that this must have been done at no very remote date.

I thought little more of the matter at the time, and was still very proud of my possession. After all, one leaf only out of nearly a hundred was not genuine; and like a man who is unwilling to face an unpleasant truth, I used to turn hastily past that leaf when I displayed the book to visitors in future.

No ephemeral literature approaches in fascination a book seller's catalogue. To receive one at the breakfast-table, skim through it with one's bacon and eggs, send off a postcard by the first mail for some long-sought rarity - or even a telegram if circumstances demand it - these are among the highest pleasures of life. Nor can I bring myself to throw away a catalogue when it is out of date, until a mountainous accumulation of them demands some drastic action. Then perhaps once in three years - there is a gigantic sorting; some arc earmarked to be retained permanently as works of reference; the rest are reluctantly destroyed after any item of particular interest has been cut out and transferred to scrapbook.

It is my custom to browse among my old catalogues, and it was in this way that I hit upon a description of my manuscript. I was looking through a bound volume of old catalogues of the house of Leighton, a great firm in the early years of the century, but now extinct. Listed here was undoubtedly my Book of Hours; from the description of the decoration, the miniatures, and the binding it could be none other. There were, however, two points of difference. In the first place the coat-of-arms at the beginning had been intact in 1904, the date of the catalogue. Unfortunately it was merely described as 'an unidentified coat-of-arms'; but it had not been erased. The second difference was more striking - I will quote front the printed description:

"Eleven of the twelve miniatures are well-executed examples of fifteenth-century Flemish illumination, but the twelfth, illustrating the Burial Service, is by another hand. It is a crude but vivid drawing in pen and ink of a church interior. In the foreground two figures are assisting in the Raising of Lazarus, watched by a seated figure in one of the pews; a fourth figure, apparently a priest, is depicted as running through the door of the church . It is difficult to account for this variation from the normal representation of the scene, which is apparently nearly contemporary with the rest of the manuscript."

Here was a very curious problem. Why should anyone in the last twenty years have destroyed this miniature, and substituted a modern imitation of the Orthodox version of the Raising of Lazarus? Why, too, should anyone have erased the arms? I was sufficiently interested to attempt to find the answer to this puzzle.

I first tried to trace the previous owner. At the sale in I which I bought it, the book had been described as 'The Property of a Gentleman,' and the auctioneers would not, naturally, disclose the identity of their client. Next I got the address of Clarkson, the illuminator, from my friend at the Museum, and went to see him. He recognised the book and admitted the authorship of the modern miniature. The one which it had replaced had already been cut out when he received the volume; and the arms had been erased. I asked him for the name of the man who had commissioned the work, and after some hesitation he gave it to me. It was that of a Cornish antiquary with some of whose published work I was familiar. I wrote to him, telling him what I already knew of the circumstances, and asking him if he would be kind enough to satisfy my curiosity in the matter. I received a rebuff. I will quote from his letter.

"You are correct in your deduction that I was the previous owner of the Book of Hours in your possession, and that I destroyed the miniature and had another one substituted. I am fully aware that such an act must appear to you to be a piece of wanton vandalism; nevertheless I am not prepared to defend it or even to discuss it. Let it suffice that my reasons to my own mind were entirely adequate and that my own conscience is clear on the matter..."

There seemed to be nothing more that I could do. It was extremely irksome to have an unexplained mystery on my shelves, but I could not force the man to tell me about it and presumably he had some good reason for his reticence. About a year ago he died, and I received from his executors a sealed envelope bearing my name in his handwriting. It contained several closely written sheets of foolscap and a covering letter:

"Dear Mr -----, I have decided that after all you should know the story connected with your Book or Hours. I purchased it in 1904 from the firm of Leighton and was intrigued by the extraordinary miniature illustrating the Burial Service. I succeeded in discovering what lay behind it, and I wish to God that I had never done so. Since that day I have never seen the book without a shudder - funerals have filled me with an unreasoning dread and the thought of my own with a mortal terror. It was for my own peace of mind that I destroyed the miniature, and I obliterated the arms which gave me the clue to the story. They were the arms of Prior Ralph Tregannet, the last Prior of the small Benedictine Priory of St Fagan, near Fowey in Cornwall, which was dissolved in 1536. I discovered the monastic records of this Priory among some of the archives of the great Benedictine House of Milton Abbey in Dorset, now in a private collection. Amongst them were certain papers of the last Prior from which I was able to reconstruct the story which I give below. When you have read it you will perhaps understand how powerfully the miniature worked on my imagination, and will blame me less for the destruction of an eyewitness's picture of a scene of unexampled horror…"

You can imagine with what interest I picked up the foolscap sheet and started to read.

"The ancient family of Tregannet were Lords of the Manor of St Deniol in Cornwall from time immemorial until the beginning of the eighteenth century, when the line became extinct. The present Manor House, which I have visited, dates from the early seventeenth century, but it is built on the foundations of a very much earlier structure. In the turbulent history of the county the name of Tregannet is ever to the fore, and Hector Tregannet, born in 1452, was no exception. Like so many West Country gentlemen he was an active Lancastrian and fought as a young man at Tewkesbury. In the rising of 1479, though a man of forty-five, he was one of the hot-heads who, having marched the whole length of Southern England, met their defeat at Deptford Strand. Here Tregannet received the King's Pardon and returned to his estates. But this firebrand did not confine himself to disturbing the peace of his king; he was likewise a scourge to his neighbours. Like so many of his fellow Cornishmen, he turned his hand to piracy, and the curious can find in the Patent Rolls an account of his depredations from Fowey upon the shipping of the Breton ports. Tregannet was, in short, just such a man as one would expect to flourish in the absence of a strong government, an opportunist who made the most of a period of feudal anarchy and social unrest. His son, the Prior, might be expected to put forward his better qualities, yet even in his son's narrative he appears a reckless, overbearing man who would stop short of no crime to achieve his ends - not even murder.

"The Tregannet lands were fairly extensive and included a rugged stretch of coast between St Austell and Fowey. To the east were the Church lands of the the Priory of St Fagan and in the priory church were the tombs of past generations of Tregannets. To the north lay the small estate of a yeoman farmer named Thomas Prest. Between the families of Prest and Tregannet there was a feud, the origins of which went back to some boundary dispute of remote antiquity. Thomas Prest appears to have been an upright, resolute man, who refused to be intimidated by his more powerful neighbour. He would seem to have acted with great moderation under considerable provocation, for on several occasions his cattle had been driven off and his servants assaulted and in those times of civil war it was hard to obtain any legal redress. His estate, though not large, was a good one, and Hector Tregannet had for many years cast covetous eyes upon it. In the year 1502 he succeeded in incorporating it within the Manor of St Deniol by methods of peculiar ruthlessness. The Prior's narrative is slightly ambiguous, but there is little doubt that he circulated in the surrounding countryside dark stories of witchcraft, which finally so inflamed the minds of the superstitious peasantry that one night they went in a body to Prest's house and fired it. Tregannet himself watched the outrage with every sign of satisfaction. Prest and his wife - they were childless - were trapped in an upper room, but the crowd made no attempt to rescue them. As they stood round the blazing building, the smoke cleared for a moment and the form of Thomas Prest could be seen at the window. He recognised Tregannet below, and after calling upon God to bear witness to his innocence, he set a curse upon his enemy, 'that he would never be buried with his forefathers in the Priory Church of St Fagan.' The smoke eddied up again and he was seen no more. Both he and his wife perished in the gutted building, and in default of an heir his lands were seized by the Tregannets.

"The conscience of Hector Tregannet did not, however, rest easy. He could not forget the curse put upon him by the neighbour whom he had wronged. He went abroad less than he had done and abandoned his piratical enterprises, for he was resolved to die in his bed and find his last resting place with his forefathers.

"In 1510 he died. At his deathbed his two sons swore that they would bury him in the Priory Church - he thought that he had cheated the curse.

"The day of the funeral was hot and airless, and the sky overcast. An oppressive atmosphere of expectation lay like a pall over the countryside. The coffin of Hector Tregannet was slowly carried from his house into the Priory Church and set down before the choir steps. The nave was full of the dead man's tenants, and in the choir were the ten monks of the establishment and six of the lay brothers. As the voice of the officiating priest chanted the Burial Service, the heat became more and more stifling and the interior of the church became darker. Just as he reached the words, "Memento, homo, quia pulvis es et in pulverem revertis" there was a sudden vivid flash of lightning and a single clap of thunder right overhead. The congregation was half blinded by the flash, but when their eyes were accustomed to the gloom once more, they saw two figures standing on the choir steps, one on each side of the coffin. And as one man the congregation and the monks rose and ran headlong from the church, even the priest who had been reading the service.

And as they ran, torrential rain began to fall with a continuous roaring sound. But the younger son of the dead man did not run away, because he was lame. He tried to avert his eyes from the two figures on the choir steps, but he could not. And he saw that they were blind, for their faces were charred and shapeless, and the arms with which they groped and fumbled at the coffin ended in blackened stumps.

"He must have fainted, for he remembered no more until he found two monks bending over him. Several hours had passed before any of them had found the courage to return. Of the figures there was no sign and the coffin was empty. The body of Hector Tregannet was never seen again by human eye.

"The younger son devoted the rest of his days to the service of God; he entered the Benedictine Order and eventually became the last Prior of St Fagan's. He gave the estate of Thomas Prest to the Church. And as an act of penance for his father's sins, to keep ever fresh in his mind the dangers of incurring the Divine Wrath, he set down on vellum the scene in the Priory Church, and substituted it for the Flemish miniature of the Raising of Lazarus in his Book of Hours."

AN ENCOUNTER
IN THE MIST

I am in the fortunate position of having a good deal of leisure. This, however, has its disadvantages. My family is a large one and has never been backward in calling upon my services, and if ever a trustee or an executor is required my name is the first that springs to mind. I assume this is because I have plenty of time on my hands, for I am hardly vain enough to think that I have any aptitude for worldly affairs. But whatever the cause, I not infrequently find myself clearing up the estates and going through the papers of some deceased relative, generally a dull and thankless task. The papers of my late maternal uncle Giles, who died in 1912, looked like proving no exception.

He had achieved some small distinction as a geologist in the 'scvcntic's of the last century – I believe his monograph on the fossils of the Middle Chalk was a standard text-book in its day. I had painstakingly arranged for the disposal of his belongings, and had managed to persuade the Natural History Museum at South Kensington to accept eleven large cabinets of geological specimens. His letters and papers I had removed to my flat, and was examining them at my leisure. They were copious and extremely uninteresting, and it was only by exercise of considerable will-power that I persevered to the end. I am exceedingly glad that I did so, for embedded in a diary recording the humdrum affairs of the year 1879 I came upon the narrative of an event unique even in my experience of uncommon events. Uncle Giles obviously appreciated the startling nature of what befell him, for be recorded the incidents in the greatest detail, as one would expect from a man of science. He confined himself, however, to the facts, and failed to comment upon them. The narrative below is reconstructed from the diary, and I have only omitted a number of passages of a geological nature and of no interest to the general reader.

In October 1879 Giles Hampton, then in his middle thirties, was spending a short holiday in Wales. A friend of his, Beverley by name, had recently retired from his business in Liverpool, and had built himself a house in Caernarvonshire, on a lower slope of the Snowdon range. His invitation to stay had been especially welcome as his house was an admirable centre for a number of geological excursions. Giles arrived at Fablan Fawr, as the property was called, on the evening of October 10th. The house was extremely comfortable by the standards of the 'seventies - it possessed, in fact, one of the first bathrooms to be installed in the county.

Although its architecture would hardly satisfy modern taste, my uncle waxed enthusiastic over its noble yellow-brick turrets commanding the valley below. It was certainly placed in a splendid setting right at the head of a re-entrant in the hills. From the terrace in front of it one looked down over the Conway Valley, while immediately behind it the mountains proper began; the crest of the range being about seven miles away. The house lay at the upper extremity of the cultivated zone, and a few hundred yards from the garden began the rocky heather-covered slopes of the hillside.

The weather was good, and for the first week of his stay Giles accompanied Beverley on a number of excursions - on two days they shot, and on others they visited various neighbours and beauty spots in the district. His diary begins to reflect a fear that his social activities will prevent him from making the geological expeditions he had planned. On October 18th, however, his host had business to transact in the local market-town, and Giles took the opportunity to make an all-day excursion to some large slate quarries which lay some ten miles away on the far side of the range of hills. The sky was overcast but gave promise of improvement later when Giles set off after an early breakfast. In his haversack were his luncheon and his geological hammer, and he had received from the groom a minute description of the best route to follow across the range.

It is a commonplace that a journey in hills takes longer than one anticipates, and it was after twelve o'clock when Giles reached his destination. The sun had come out and he was hot and tired though much encouraged by the interest of the quarries he had come to see. So absorbing did he find them and so full were the notes he took, that it was not until half-past three that he started on the return journey: By this time the sun had clouded over again and it looked like rain. As he re-ascended the track into the hills, a fine drizzle began to fall which increased as he reached the higher altitudes, and before he had climbed to the crest he was enveloped in a thick mist, which reduced visibility first to a few yards and finally to n few feet only. My uncle had carefully noted various landmarks on his path, and even in the mist was confident of keeping to the right track. The route, however, was ill-defined, being in places little more than a steep track, and when Giles found himself crossing an unfamiliar stream, he had to confess that he had strayed from the correct path. He retraced his footsteps for nearly half a mile, but failed to return to a point he had noted where the track ran between two prominent rocks. Then indeed be realised that he was lost in earnest.

He sat down for a few moments to consider his position. It was not the prospective discomfort of a night on the hillside that alarmed him, but the certainty that Beverley must be seriously upset by his non-appearance. Above all, he hated making a nuisance of himself. He pictured the assembling of a search party from every cottage on the estate and the upheaval in the well ordered existence of his host. With this in mind one can appreciate how relieved he was to hear the sound of a dog's bark and footsteps in the mist on the hillside above him - footsteps interspersed with the tapping of a stick. He shouted and a voice in Welsh answered him. From out of the mist came the figure of an old man, with a great collie at his heels. Although old, he bore, himself well. He wore a cloak of some dark material which reached to his ankles, but was bareheaded. His hair, which was long and white, framed a red wrinkled face which radiated kindliness and benevolence.

He spoke again in Welsh, and when Giles, by his gestures, showed him that he could not understand he smiled reassuringly. Giles indicated that he was lost which was indeed pretty obvious, and repeated three or four times the name of his friend's estate, Fablan Fawr. The old man smiled again and nodded vigorously; then plunging his hand into the fold of his cloak he brought out a map, which he spread on a stone before him. Beverley's newly built house was not, of course, marked upon it, but it showed clearly the church situated a few hundred yards below it.

With a gnarled forefinger the stranger indicated on the map the spot at which they were standing and then traced slowly the track Giles must follow to reach his destination. This he did three times, making sure that my uncle thoroughly understood the route. Then refolding the map, he pressed it into his hearer's hands. Giles tried to refuse the gift, but the old man only laughed and nodded. So thanking him profusely, the lost wayfarer set out along the route he had been shown having gone a few yards, he turned and saw the figure standing, dimly discernible in the mist and gathering dusk, watching him. He waved his hand in farewell, took another few steps and when he next looked round, his guide was invisible.

Giles travelled rapidly to make up for lost time. The mist, if anything, had become thicker but the track which he was following was well marked, and by constant reference to the map, he made good progress and had soon crossed the ridge, and was glad to find himself on the downgrade once more. Here the path followed what seemed to be a dry streambed, which led him down the hillside at a steep, almost a precipitous angle. With the visibility at only a few feet it required to be taken cautiously. Suddenly my uncle missed his footing and stumbled - a mishap which in all probability saved his life. In his fall he dislodged a small round rock, which rolled quickly away from him - he heard it gather momentum and go clattering over a few yards of the track; then the sound ceased. Several seconds later he heard a crash, hundreds of feet below. The path had led him to the very brink of a sheer drop. Giles experimented with a further stone, with the same result; he looked again at his map, but there could be no mistake. He was sure that he had followed explicitly the course indicated to him. For the first time he became seriously alarmed. Ho realised the folly of any further move and sat disconsolately on a boulder. There was nothing for it but to wait and hope that the mist would clear, he thought, and lit his pipe.

It was perhaps an hour later that he heard faint shouts on the hillside below, shouts which he answered with all the power of his lungs. Gradually the voices came nearer and he recognised that of Beverley's coachman. He and the groom had become alarmed for the safety of the guest and had set out to find him. Beverley himself had not yet returned home, for which Giles was profoundly thankful. The two servants escorted my uncle along the top of the cliff to a point where they rejoined the path down to the house, and in not much more than an hour he was changing his wet clothes none the worse for his adventure. Something prompted him to say nothing of his strange encounter on the hillside to his rescuers nor did he mention this part of the story to his host at dinner-time. He told him, however, that he had strayed in the mist and had found himself on the edge of the cliff.

"You had a damned lucky escape," said Beverley. "There have been some nasty accidents in these hills. There was a man killed about four years ago, jus before I came here. I believe he was found at the foot of the very cliff where you nearly came to grief." He turned to the butler, "You'd remember it, Parry,"' he said. "Wasn't that the place?"

"Indeed it was, sir," replied the butler; "a gentleman from London he was, and buried in the churchyard of the village here. I was in service with Captain Trefor the Fron that time, and he gave us the afternoon off for the funeral. The Reverend Roberts buried him - powerful in prayer he was that day. I've kept a piece from the paper till today - from the *Caernarfon and District Advertiser*. I'll fetch it, if you like, sir."

Beverley assented, and after a few minutes the butler returned with a newspaper cutting. Beverley and my uncle read the trite phrases of the local journalist, dated June 6th;

"Early on Wednesday morning last the body of a young man was found at the foot of the cliffs near Adwy-yr-Eryron pass, examination of which revealed that the deceased had been dead for some hours. The remains have been identified as being those of John Stephenson, a young legal gentleman of London, who was visiting Llanberis on holiday, and who had set forth on Tuesday morning to explore the splendours or our Cambrian fastness and did not return that night. Wilson Jones, Esq., M.P., with the public spirit which characterises his every action, organised a search party, but their efforts were hampered by the inclemency of the elements. It would appear that the deceased wandered from his path in the mist, plunged over the precipice into oblivion, and was thus cut off in his prime. A member of the party who made the sad discovery has informed our correspondent that the unhappy wayfarer had in his possession a long-obsolete map of the hills, upon which was marked the disused track across the ridge rendered dangerous by the great landslide of 1852, which carried away whole sections of the path, a cataclysmic occurrence that can still be remembered by some of the older members of the community. The use of such a map must be regarded as a contributory cause of the catastrophe. Let the future explorers of our barren hills take heed from the sad demise of this young person, and recall the solemn thought, applicable alike to those of high and low degree, that in the midst of life we are in death. A modern, accurate and well-engraved folding map of the area (mounted on linen, with panorama, *1s. 6d.*; on paper without panorama, *9d.*) can be obtained from the offices of our journal."[1]

The reference to the obsolete map found on the body excited considerable speculation in my uncle's brain. The coincidence was really too extraordinary to keep to himself and he felt impelled to tell his host the whole story. Beverley was deeply interested.

"Do you remember anything about a map Parry?" he asked, addressing the butler again.

"Indeed I do sir," replied the butler, 'Very old-fashioned it was. The Reverend Roberts has it down at the Vicarage."

"In that case," said Beverley, "would you send down to Mr Roberts, give him my compliments, and ask if it would be convenient for him to come and drink his coffee with us. And ask him if he would be kind enough to bring the map with him."

The servant hurried off to do his bidding.

"The map given to me is in my pocket," said Giles. "I'll go and get it."

He fetched it and having spread it on the table, the two men pored over it. In the mist my uncle had noticed nothing odd about it but in the brightly lit dining-room it had a very unusual aspect. The engraving bad a rude archaic look, the lettering of the place names employed the long 's' and the paper was yellow with age. It was Beverley who first noted the inscription at the foot, engraved m a neat copperplate script – 'Madog ap Rhys, 1707.'

The arrival of the vicar put an end to their expressions of surprise and incredulity. He listened with the greatest attention to my uncle's tale and produced from his pocket the duplicate of the map that lay on the table.

"I've always been puzzled how such a map came to be upon the body," he said. "It's a very rare piece of engraving. The only other example I know is in the National Library of Wales."

"And who was Madog ap Rhys?" asked Giles.

"He was a hermit," replied the vicar, "who lived up on the hillside. I can show you the remains of his cell. He died in 1720. In those days they were working the lead down in Cwm Cadfan, and the ridge was crossed a great deal more frequently than it is now. Madog ap Rhys made it his special care to seek out lost travellers and guide them to safety, and whenever the mist was down he would wander along the range with his dog. He drew out and had engraved the map which we have before us, to present to wayfarers who had missed their path. There is a local superstition that he is still to be seen on the hillside, but I must confess that until today I have never taken it very seriously."

Such is the story of my uncle Giles's adventure, and I trust that the reader will agree with me as to its unique quality. Malevolent spirits who lead travellers to their death are common to the folklore of all nations and all periods, but in a very different category is this case of the ghost of a benevolent hermit, who revisited the scene of his former acts of kindness and, with the best intentions in the world, inadvertently sent unsuspecting wanderers to their destruction.

THE
LECTERN

I was on holiday. During the previous fortnight I had been driving slowly westward, with many leisurely halts to explore the book and antique dealers' shops on the way. The back of the car was filled to overflowing with the gleanings of my visits to Reading, Oxford, Cheltenham and Hereford. A big portfolio of brass rubbings and an old-fashioned plate camera bore testimony to hours passed in the parish churches of Berkshire and Gloucestershire. At Hereford I had spent several days renewing my acquaintance with the Carrick relics in the Old House, and examining the small chained library in the parish church, which tends to get overlooked. It cannot vie with the magnificent collection of chained books in the cathedral, but it well repaid the afternoon I'd devoted to it. I took several photographs, and left the plates to be developed in the town, in tending to return that way. I had no timetable and no plans. It would be a full ten days before I had to return to London, so I studied the map and the guide-books - an enthralling occupation. Two courses attracted me - either to Strike north to Ludlow and Shrewsbury or west into Wales. After some deliberation, I chose the latter; I knew Ludlow fairly well, and wanted to break fresh ground. I had heard that Llanthony Abbey was well worth a visit, and it had the added attraction in my eyes of having an association with Walter Savage Landor, one of my many interests.

It was not until after lunch on a glorious September afternoon that I set out from Hereford. I drove slowly with the car roof open, and turned onto the main road at St Devereux to see the Late Norman church at Kilpeck. I was so intrigued by the elaborate ornamental sculpture, curiously Scandinavian in its appearance, that I did not regain the main road until tea-time. Obviously Llanthony Abbey could not be visited that afternoon, so I began to think of finding a place to spend the night. Ahead of me were the Black Mountains, looking anything but sinister in the warm rays of the September sun. Obeying an impulse, I turned off to the right short of them and entered the Golden Valley.

The name caught my eye on the map, and I felt that this El Dorado in the Marches should be explored. It was a pleasant enough valley, though it hardly seemed to justify its name. I did not, however, penetrate more than a few miles along it, but turned down a lane on my left, at the end of which was a signpost which said - GRELYN 3½ miles. The lane twisted and turned and climbed steadily. I passed a few cottages, but as I approached the hills the countryside became more deserted. The road surface got worse until it was little better than a stony track. I was beginning to doubt the existence of Grelyn when, having skirted a low wooded spur, the lane ended in a tiny hamlet. It lay on my left under the hills at the head of a small valley. A little stream ran down and filled a small pool - no doubt the drinking pool, or *grelyn*, from which the place took its name. There was a church, a house that was obviously the vicarage, three cottages and an inn. Across the stream I could see indistinctly through the trees a ruin of some sort. The Prandle Arms was one of those clean, unpretentious country inns which abound in the British Isles. The single guest-room, in which I put my bag, was light and airy. It was above the front porch and looked out over the lane down which I had driven. I could see from the greater elevation of the bedroom window the ruined stone house on the other side of the little valley, and I noticed that it could be approached by a footpath that crossed the stream by a crude plank bridge. I went downstairs and had a cup of tea in the parlour, discussing an evening meal with the innkeeper's wife, an obliging woman, who offered to produce some freshly caught trout at eight o'clock. Through the window I caught a glimpse of the innkeeper himself, working in his vegetable garden. It was not yet six and I strolled out to take the air. The church, my first objective, was rather disappointing – a featureless solid building in the austere style of the Transitional period, much restored in the middle of the last century.

The monuments were ordinary in the extreme. One tablet caught my eye on account of its unusual text, and a restraint so unlike most of the florid memorial of its date:

T.P.
Ob.3I Oct. MDCCXCVII AET.23
A BIRD OF THE AIR SHALL CARRY THE
VOICE
AND THAT WHICH HATH WINGS SHALL
TELL OF THE MATTER
Ecc.x.2o

But there was little else to detain me. I walked on down the footpath that crossed the stream, and made my way slowly through what had been the park of the house across the valley. The land had gone back sadly; what muse once have been good pasture was now a derelict wilderness of thistle and thorn, great elms lay rotting where they had fallen, and over everything lay the sad hand of decay. I passed through a little belt of trc.,., and found myself faced by a high stone wall. It was in a ruinous state, and I had only to go a few yards to my right to find a breach in it. I clambered over a heap of stone and rubble, and in front of me lay the house.

A ruined house is a moving sight, far more so than a ruined castle. The latter one *expects* to be a ruin. It is difficult for the imagination to visualise the everyday life of men and women in a castle; but a house is full of human associations. The house before me had been a fine one; a long two storeyed stone building with bold step-gables. I could see now that it was only a shell; it had been burnt out and the roof and first floor had gone. Looking up through the upper windows, I could see the sky above. A formal garden on my right hand had once been enclosed by a yew hedge, now an unkempt mass of ragged trees. Within were the remnants of a rose garden, hut all the roses had reverted to their common prototype, the coarse, tangled briar. Everything was choked with rank weeds. On the walls the ivy had run riot, strangling a great magnolia that had miraculously survived the fire.

I mounted the two steps to peer in through the cavity which had once been the front door - the interior was a blackened mass of beams and stone slabs from the roof. I walked round the house; at the can end was a little oriel window. At the back I had a surprise. There was a small chapel, detached from the main building by a gap of a few yards; but it had not escaped the fire. The doorway was blocked by a heap of fallen masonry from the roof, and I peered through one of the unglazed windows. There was little to be seen. Here, too, the ivy had cloaked everything with its ubiquitous tendrils. On the walls were several tablets, nearly obscured by moss. On two of them I made out the name Prandle.

I was by now feeling hungry, and looked at my watch. It said twenty to eight, and I hastily retraced my steps. As I walked back along the path to the stream, I pondered on the history of the place. The house, l thought, had been built about 1600, and it was possible that the chapel was a little earlier. I decided to ask the innkeeper about it after supper.

I did so, but he had little to tell me. He was a silent, taciturn man, and seemed to become even more reserved when I raised the ruined house as a topic of conversation. It had belonged, he said, to a family named Prandle, and had been burned down rather over a hundred years ago. Since then no one had bought the property or farmed the land. More than that he could not or would not tell me. The night was fine and still, and I thought l would smoke my last pipe in the open air before turning in. I sauntered slowly down the footpath to the stream, and sat for a while upon the handrail of the little bridge. I could dimly discern the form of the house in the trees, standing out a little blacker than the blackness of the hillside behind it.

An owl was calling up there among the trees; at least I supposed it was an owl. It had an eerie, half-human sound that caused me to shiver slightly. For some reason my mind harked back to the text on the wall of the church. Then I half smiled to myself. I was becoming a prey to the gloomy atmosphere of the place. It called again - a little closer this time. It was like no owl that I had ever heard. Suddenly I heard a voice behind me, unmistakably human, shouting my name. I turned and saw the innkeeper at the far end of the footpath. He held a lantern in his hand which he waved to and fro. He called to me again with a note of urgency and insistence in his voice that surprised me. I shouted in answer and walked quickly up the path to meet him. As I have said, he was a dour, silent man, but there was something quite elusive about his obvious satisfaction in seeing me.

"I didn't see you go out," he said, "and we thought that maybe you'd gone up to the house again. I came to find you."

I explained that I'd been sitting on the little bridge.

"What if I had gone up to the house?" I asked. "Is there any reason why I shouldn't do so?"

"No one goes there after dark," he replied. "It gave me a rare shock when my missus said she thought she'd seen you setting off down the footpath."

"But why?' I protested. "Is the place haunted or something?"

He made no reply and I repeated the question.

"There's some things that are better not talked about," he said gruffly, relapsing into his old manner, "and Prandle Court's one of them. If you want to go nosing into things that don't concern you, you'd better ask the Vicar tomorrow. Maybe he'll tell you, for I won't. And now I'll be locking up if you don't mind."

I went indoors and he stumped off. And as I went to bed I resolved to call on the Vicar early next morning. It was ten o'clock when I presented myself at the Vicarage, and in the bright sunlight the curious events of the previous night had assumed an air of unreality. A maid showed me into the study and went in search of her master. As is my wont, I examined the books on the walls. A glance at a man's library is often an indication of the sort of man one has to deal with. These, however, did not tell me much - they were mainly theological works of the last century, with a fair number of classical texts and translations - obviously a churchman of the old school. My speculations were interrupted by the entrance of the object of them. He was a tall, elderly man, rather bald, dressed in a shabby suit of clerical grey. He shook me by the hand, offered me a chair and then looked at me enquiringly.

I had debated in my mind how I should approach the subject and, rejecting the idea of any elaborate circumlocution, I had decided to be perfectly frank. In a few words I told him of my experience of the night before, and the curiosity which it had aroused in me. I said a little of my interest in the supernatural, and asked him whether he would be good enough to tell me the history of the house.

He looked at me shrewdly for a few seconds and then said, "Yes, I will tell you, if you really wish to hear it. I suppose that it's better that I should do so than that you should ferret it out from one of the cottagers. The affair has grown into a local legend, but I happen to know the facts as well as any man. My great-grandfather was Vicar here at the time.

"The Prandle family lived in this valley from the very earliest times," he began, "and you can find the name again and again in the parish registers. In the sixteenth century the family became a prosperous one, and built Prandle Court. Previously they had been hard-working sheep-farmers, but from that time on they assumed the status of small gentry. They didn't go out into the world much - for one thing they weren't a prolific family with scores of younger sons. Occasionally, one would become a Canon of Hereford or an attorney there, but the head of one family was content to live on here at Grelyn and supervise his estate, which by the eighteenth century had become quite a large one.

"Thomas Prandle, of whom I'm going to tell you, was a man of rather a different stamp. He was born in 1774, and had been sent to Oxford, an innovation in the normal family procedure. The sons usually had a tutor at home or went to school in Hereford. By all accounts he was a pretty wild young man - though no worse, I suppose, than hundreds of others at that date. He got into some sort of trouble at the University and came down without taking a degree. After this his father kept a strict eye on him, and he spent his time helping with the estate work. It wasn't a bad life for a young man; he got plenty of hunting and shooting; but it didn't suit Thomas Prandle. The glimpse he had gut at Oxford of the life of the *beau-monde* had left him unfitted for playing the squire in a place like Grelyn. He was bored to tears. He wanted to go into the army, but his father wouldn't let him, because he was the heir.

"You can imagine with what joy a young man like this greeted Pill's raising of the 'Fencibles' in 1793 - the locally organised forces which were to take over home defence. He quickly got a Commission in a local regiment of Volunteer Horse, and devoted himself heart and soul to making the local farmers' sons into passable troopers. For over three years they did their drills and manoeuvres. In February 1797 they got their first taste of excitement when a small force of French landed at Fishguard, only to surrender a few hours later. Thomas handle's regiment didn't get on the scene soon enough to have any part in their capture, but they guarded the prisoners as far as Hereford.

"The following month the rumour came that they were going overseas, and Prandle was wild with excitement. He pictured himself getting to grips with the French at last. The truth was far more humdrum. The regiment was destined for Ulster, where disorder had spread throughout the province, following the appearance of a French Beet in Bantry Bay. The very small regular forces on the spot couldn't deal with the situation, and Lord Camden sent for reinforcements. General Lake arrived with a mixed force of Militia and Volunteer regiments, and received orders to disarm the province.

"It very soon became clear to Prandle and his troop that this wasn't the glamorous business for which they'd been training so long. Instead of the dashing cavalry charge that he'd pictured he found the drab necessity of conducting house-to-house searches in a hostile countryside. There is no glory for the soldier matched against guerrillas - no enemy drawn up in line to do battle, only a sordid series of murdered sentries, shots in the dark and vanishing assailants. The inevitable reprisals only made a bad situation worse. The soldier is at an enormous disadvantage in dealing with civilians. If he is a man of chivalry, they can insult him with impunity, for he cannot retaliate. If an unarmed man is killed by a soldier there is an immediate outcry. The Irish were past masters at the art of civil disorder, and made the most of the inexperience of their assailants.

"Under the strain of these conditions the discipline of some of these Volunteer regiments slackened woefully. After all, they were not highly trained regular troops, but a very mixed collection of amateurs, sometimes indifferently officered. Small bands of troops roamed the countryside conducting searches on their own account - any form of resistance or even expostulation meant the burning of the house. When the soldiers found drink any outrage might be committed. Thomas Prandle's troop got itself a pretty bad name. He was a very young excitable man, and no disciplinarian; moreover both his men and himself were not infrequently the worse for liquor.

"Only one of the acts of barbarism which they committed concerns us today. They went up one night to search a small village in the hills near Newry, where it was suspected that arms were bidden. They found no arms, but quantities of poteen. During the revels that ensued, a trooper was wounded by n shot from a window, and by the time his fuddled companions had gathered their wits the would-be assassin had disappeared. All hell broke loose in the village half of it was burned down, including the church. The terrified villagers tried to save some of the fittings, and a small brazen eagle-lectern caught Prandle's eye, among a litter of vestments, altar-candlesticks and books which lay strewn about the churchyard. Obeying some absurd whim of a drunken man, he picked it up and threw it into the light cart belonging to the troop, which accompanied search parties to carry off their spoil.

"They took their departure soon afterwards, leaving the villagers to put out the fires and to bury several dead. As the troop came down from the hills on to the main road, it fell in with a commissariat wagon train. The sergeant in charge of it was a Hereford man, known to Prandle. Still far from sober, he transferred the lectern to the wagon train and gave his friend, the sergeant, half a guinea to send it home for him. The man executed his commission well; by some devious and irregular method it was conveyed by military transport to Belfast and across the Irish Channel, thence by carrier to Prandle Court. Its arrival was the occasion of some surprise, as Thomas Prandle had made no mention of its despatch in his infrequent letters home. It was, however, placed in the family chapel, pending some explanation.

"Thomas Prandle's military career did not last very much longer. A series of outrages had made necessary an enquiry into the discipline of the regiments policing Ulster, and he was one of the many officers who were found guilty of the grossest inefficiency and neglect of duty. In less than three months he found himself at home again, chafing at the dull existence under his father's roof.

"The end of this account will sound to you like a fantasy. Frankly I don't know what to think about it. If you turn the cold light of reason on it, it sounds absurd, but · there is no doubt that my great-grandfather believed it implicitly - and he was a devout, God-fearing man, and no fool.

"A few weeks after Thomas Prandle's return, there was a disturbance in the night at the house. Several of the servants said subsequently that they thought they had heard a cry in the early hours of the morning. The son of the house did not appear at breakfast-time. His room was empty and a search was instituted. It was not necessary to look far. The door of the chapel was open, and a servant, who looked in, was horrified to see the young man lying on the stone floor by the altar steps under the lectern. He was dead and had been the object of an attack of peculiar bestiality. His face in particular had been terribly mutilated. Some of the household thought that his assailant had been human, others some wild beast, possibly a wild cat or even a wolf, though such a thing had not been heard of in Wales for hundreds of years. But my great-grandfather the Vicar, who was quickly summoned, knew at once what had killed Thomas Prandle; for as a young man he'd visited the Holy Land and had seen the body of a man after the vultures had settled upon it.

'No motive for his having gone into the chapel by night was ever discovered. It was very little used, as the family always attended the church at Grelyn. Thomas Prandle was buried there, and a small memorial tablet was put up by my great grandfather.

"The eagle-lectern was packed up and sent off to Ireland; but it never arrived. That autumn the gales blew with unusual fury in the Channel, and the Irish packet foundered off Belfast. Since that date misfortune dogged the family of Prandle. The shock of his son's death killed the old man, and not many years later the house was burned down. A cousin inherited the place, but never came near it, and most of the land has been sold off. It has never been possible to find a tenant for the home-park and gardens. Country people have long memories, and there were all sorts of local tales of things seen and heard near the house alter dark. I can't vouch for them myself, for though I've been here twenty-five years I've never been over there after nightfall. You may think I'm a superstitious old fool, but I believe in letting sleeping dogs lie. For if places *are* haunted, I can't think of any more suitable place than Prandle Court."

NUMBER
SEVENTY-NINE

"I'm sorry, sir, but number seventy-nine isn't available."

The bookseller's young assistant shook his head complacently as be pronounced the words. I was bitterly disappointed. It wasn't as though I had wasted any time. The catalogue had reached my breakfast-table only a half an hour before, and I had gulped down my coffee and made a beeline for Edgerton's bookshop, an old firm whose premises were situated in one of the passages just off Red Lion Square. The item which had so aroused my interest was a manuscript of the mid-seventeenth century, dealing with the sombre subject of necromancy. From the cataloguer's description it seemed possible to me that it was a transcript of one of the lost manuscripts of Dr John Dee, the Elizabethan astrologer. If this were the case, the price of fifteen pounds was by no means excessive, and I had set my heart on securing the book. Hence my disappointment.

"Was it sold before the catalogue was sent out?" I asked.

The young man shook his head again.

"If it's been ordered but is still on the premises. Perhaps I could see it?" I continued eagerly.

The assistant seemed em harassed. "I am afraid it isn't available," he repeated evasively. "I can't tell you any more than that." Then his face lit up with relief. "Ah, here is Mr Egerton coming in now," he said. "You'd better ask him about it."

I turned to greet the proprietor as he came through the shop door.

"What's all this mystery about number seventy-nine?" I said, waving my catalogue at him. "I gather it hasn't been sold yet. Can I have a look at it? Surely that's not much to ask, after all the years I've dealt with you."

The bookseller's usually genial face clouded over, and he hesitated before replying. Finally he said, "Will you come upstairs to my room?"

I accompanied him through the shop and past the little cataloguer's room behind it, and we mounted the stairs together. I'd always liked the firm of Egerton. The bulk of their business was in legal books, but their catalogues usually had something in them of interest to me, and over a period of fifteen years I'd bought a number of books from them. Egerton himself had become quite a personal friend. We often met in the reading-room of the British Museum. We entered his room on the first floor lined with reference books, and he waved me into a chair,

"The manuscript you want to see has been destroyed." he said.

"I'm very sorry to hear that," I replied. "What an unfortunate accident!"

"It wasn't an accident," he said abruptly. "It was burned by - myself."

I looked at him. He was obviously upset and reluctant to discuss the matter, but why on earth a business man like Egerton should have destroyed a book worth fifteen pounds was beyond my comprehension. He realised that some explanation was clue, but seemed to be undecided whether to give it to me. Finally he said, "I'll tell you about it, if you like. In fact, it's rather more in your line than mine."

He paused, and I waited hopefully.

"You knew Merton?" he resumed.

"Your cataloguer?" I said. "Why, of course I know him you've had him with you for years."

Merton was one of those enigmatic figures that one occasionally meets in the rare-book business - a man of considerable ability and apparently not the slightest ambition.

"I don't think I've ever told you his history," said Egerton. "He came down from Oxford in 1913, and got caught up in the war before he'd settled down to anything. He was badly shell-shocked in France, and when he got his discharge in 1918 he was a nervous wreck. He came to me temporarily while he was looking round for something to do, and stayed for twenty years. Of course he was eccentric, but extremely able. In fact, he was so eccentric that I used never to let him deal with customers, but if he kept in his room behind the shop he did really excellent work. I think I can justifiably claim a very high standard for our catalogues, and this was due to Merton. Of course he was undeniably odd - he was normally moody, but sometimes he'd get fits of depression for weeks on end, during which he literally would hardly speak a word to a soul. He wasn't a very cheerful member of the firm, but his excellence at his job compensated for his other failings.

"About a year ago he came to me one morning and announced that he was engaged to be married. I was astounded, but also delighted for his sake. I felt that if anything could help him to overcome his moodiness and eccentricity, married life would do it for him. I congratulated him warmly and agreed to raise his salary. His fiancée came to the shop several times and he introduced her to me. Site struck me as being just the sort of wife he needed - about twenty-five and obviously extremely capable and sensible. He was devoted to her and became a new man. I've never seen such a transformation as his. You would never have recognised him as the shy, tongue-tied recluse that he was before."

I shifted uneasily in my chair, wondering what all this had

to do with the hook I wanted. Egerton must have sensed my unspoken impatience, for he continued, "Don't think that all this is irrelevant. You'll see soon how the manuscript fits into the story. But first I must tell you more about Merton.

"Four months ago his fiancée was killed - in a motoring accident. Naturally any man would be deeply upset in such circumstances, but you've no conception of the effect it had on Merton. All his past depression returned a hundred-fold accentuated. He'd sit in his room for hours on end with his head buried in his hands. He seemed to have lost all interest in life. I got seriously concerned about him, and tried to persuade him to see a doctor. I offered him a month's holiday by the sea, but he refused to take it. If he hadn't been such an old and tried member of the firm, I should really have had to consider getting rid of him.

"From a conversation I had with him at this time I learned that some quack medium had got hold of him and that he was attending séances. He asked me my view on spiritualism on one occasion, and from his remarks I gathered that he wasn't himself deriving much solace from it. The medium had, of course, promised that he should be put in touch with his dead fiancée, but the contact had still to be established. It was really pitiful to see a grown man taking such stuff seriously.

"Merton's state of mind was particularly unfortunate at this time, as I had bought a private library in Shropshire early in the summer. The catalogue I sent you last night represents only about half of it- I had hoped to have offered the whole collection for sale by now. I don't suppose Merton catalogued more than a third of the items. I did the rest; the boy down in the shop isn't up to such work yet. I expect you noticed a small section of occult books, of which number seventy-nine was one. Those were the only books in which Merton showed any interest - he spent hours on them, far more time than their value justified, but I didn't mind. I was so glad to see him at work again, and hoped it would be a prelude to returning to his normal output.

"One night about a week ago Merton came up to my room at closing time, and made me an offer of ten pounds for the manuscript. I was surprised at this - he wasn't a collector, and I knew that he couldn't afford it. I refused – rather brusquely, I'm afraid. When he had gone I had a good look at it. It was full of the usual cabbalistic mumbo-jumbo, the pentacle, the secrets of Solomon, and the like, but the section on necromancy, which comprised the bulk of the book, was much fuller than I've seen in other manuscripts of this class, and included a lot of the dog-Latin incantations and conjurations to be employed by the practitioner of the black art to invoke the spirits of the dead. I put it away in the safe and thought no more about it.

"The day before yesterday Merton asked me for the key of the safe at lunch-time. This was such a common occurrence that I gave it to him quite automatically, without asking him what he wanted. There are always a few good things in there awaiting cataloguing, and I assumed that be was going to make a start on one of them.

"Now, although we close at six o'clock, if I'm busy I'm very often on the premises until eight or even later. The boy goes off at six sharp, but Merton used to stay on for another half hour or so. I was always the hut to leave. That evening I was hard at work trying to trace an obscure coat-of-arms on a German binding. I never could find my way about Rietstap. It was about half-past seven, and I assumed that Merton had gone home, although I usually heard the door when he let himself out. It was, of course, quite dark outside.

"Suddenly I heard a cry from downstairs. It was Merton's voice, and I don't think I've ever heard such a degree of fear infused into a single scream; it expressed the very essence of terror. I opened my door quickly and looked down over the banisters into the well of the staircase. The switch is at the foot of the stairs and the light was off. I could hear him pulling the door handle of his room, and as I watched the door was flung open. His room too was in darkness so I got only a glimpse of what happened then; for the light coming over my shoulder from the open door behind me shone only halfway down the stairs. Merton ran through the shop, and I heard the bell ring as he opened the outer door. I was going to shout after him, when I saw something else emerge from his room.

"At least I can't say that I saw it; I thought I discerned a shadowy figure come through the doorway, but apart from an impression of grey colouring I could not describe it. But it wasn't what I saw that made me shudder, it was a smell - one that I had met only once before in my life, and that was forty years ago. When I was a boy, we had an exhumation in the village churchyard, and being an inquisitive child I crept up between the tombstones as the grave-diggers were raising the coffin. I only got a glimpse because the village policeman spotted me, and I got a clout on the side of the head for my pains. But I smelt a smell that I didn't meet again until it floated up the well of these stairs on the night before last - a dank, sickening, fetid reek of rottenness and decay. I nearly fainted with revulsion.

"In a second I was back in my room with the door shut. I sat there for a few minutes, and then I thought of Merton and wondered what had become of him. I plucked up courage and went downstairs - the place was deserted and the shop door still open. I went outside and hurried down the passage towards Holborn. I remember thinking, as I did so, how quiet everything seemed. When I emerged into Holborn I discovered the reason. The traffic was stationary and in the middle of the road a group of people were gathered round a prone figure. I pushed my way through the crowd and saw that it was Merton. A policeman told me that he had run headlong from the passage straight under the wheels of a bus, and had been killed instantly.

"You can imagine how shaken I was when I came back to the hop. I went into Merton's room and there on his desk was the damned manuscript. From the plate at which it was open and from some notes on his pad, it was obvious that the poor devil had been experimenting with one of the formulae set out there. Something had occurred to frighten him out of his wits, and in his nervous state this wasn't perhaps surprising. I suppose that some obscure telepathy communicated his panic to me - at least I prefer to believe that than credit the implications of what I thought I sensed at the foot of the stairs. Anyhow, I was taking no chances, and before I went home I burned every particle of the manuscript and of Merton's notes. I'm sorry to disappoint you, but there it is. And although I've always found occult books a lucrative sideline, it's a class of literature that I shall be avoiding for the future."

THE DEVIL'S
AUTOGRAPH

"Here's a rarity," I said, as I displayed my latest acquisition. "I don't suppose you've ever seen anything like this before. It's the devil's autograph."

I smiled as I laid the book on the table, but no answering smile crossed my companion's features. He looked, indeed, interested but deadly serious. I felt slightly nettled as I opened the volume. My little alter-dinner joke didn't seem to be going very well Blenkinsop always was a dry old stick, I thought, and I wondered what impulse had made me invite the old man to my rooms. However, I expounded my newest purchase to him. It really was an interesting book, much more interesting than a casual glance at it suggested.

An indifferently printed *Introductio in Chaldaicam liguam*, published in 1539, does not sound very exciting, but at the end was an amusing supplement entitled, *Ludovici Spoletani praecepta sive ut vulgo dicitur, Conjuratio cum subscripta Daemonis responsione*. In it was described how an Italian conjured the Prince of Darkness 'per Talion, Ansion et Amlion' to tell him whether he had in fact received the whole of an inheritance. As soon as he had written this very humdrum query, the pen was snatched from him by an invisible band which wrote an answer at a great pace. The message, which proved obstinately indecipherable, was engraved on p. 212 of my volume; the hand was spiky, abounding in letters shaped like prongs and tridents. A philologist of my acquaintance told me that it had affinities to Old Iberic. All this I explained to Blenkinsop, who listened in silence. Finally, he made a comment which struck me as being the height of fatuity.

He looked at the script closely and said, "I wonder whether

it's genuine."

He had every appearance of being in earnest, but I must confess that I laughed.

"Of course it's not genuine," I said. "The devil doesn't go about autographing pieces of paper. It's an amusing attempt of a sixteenth-century humanist to impose upon his credulous readers."

Blenkinsop gave me a penetrating glance.

"Don't you bctooswe," he said. "I don't say for one moment that the devil wrote this, but I do happen to know that it is not impossible."

I scented a story. "What makes you so certain?" I asked.

"An experience I had as a boy," he answered. "I'll tell it to you, if you like, but I don't want any comment or discussion til the end. I've made up my own mind about what I think happened, and I'm really the only person who has any knowledge of the facts. Will you hear it, under these conditions?"

I agreed readily enough, and Blenkinsop relit his pipe before he began.

"The events that I'm going to relate," he said, "took place in 1889, when I was a boy of thirteen. In that year my father, who was a doctor, died, leaving me not only without a home but almost penniless. My mother had died some ten years before. As a result of this I went to live in the West Country with an uncle - an elder brother of my father's who was a Canon of Dymchester. As far as I knew, he and my father had never been on any great terms of intimacy; at all events, I had never met him before, and you can imagine with what trepidation a small orphan of thirteen arrived at his new home. My uncle was a bachelor and was considerably older than my father. He must have been over seventy-five, was partially paralysed from a stroke which he had received several years before, and walked with some difficulty upon two sticks. He had lived alone with a single manservant for many years, and I don't suppose that the intrusion of a small boy into his household can have been welcome, to say the least. Nevertheless, he received me kindly, and that same evening we discussed my future. Had my father remained alive I was to have gone to Rugby that autumn, but my altered circumstances would not permit of this, and my uncle had decided to educate me himself and then to let me go in for an Oxford scholarship in four years' time. I, of necessity, fell in with his plans.

"I quickly settled down in my new surroundings. The house was probably early Georgian, and it overlooked the cathedral close, and though it was very dark by reason of the proximity of trees to the windows, it was roomy and well-furnished. I was given a bedroom on the first floor, next to my uncle's, and was made free of his study, the biggest room on the ground floor, lined from floor to ceiling with books, row upon row of calf, vellum and crumbling russia bindings - the library of a scholar, deeply read in the Fathers and controversialists of the early Church. The gloomy roams, the heavy mahogany furniture, the orderly existence of the old Canon and his middle-aged servant, were little to the liking of an active boy in his teens, but I knew that I had no alternative, and I realised something of the sacrifice to his privacy that the old man had made by taking me in. And so I worked away at my Latin and my Greek under his tuition, and for recreation I took long solitary walks on the Mendips. I soon realised that my uncle was something of a recluse. He no longer took services or had any share in cathedral activities. In fact, he had not been out of the house since his stroke, and took no part in the social life of the small town. A few of the married clergy with children invited me to their houses, but I soon discovered that the Canon disapproved of these visits. He did not actually forbid them, but quite obviously discouraged them, and to avoid giving offence to the old man I felt myself obliged to decline such invitations and was thrown back upon my own resources. I knew that I was an object of curiosity and some pity in the town, but I was a self-reliant child and did not care. Indeed, I took a queer sort of pride in my ability to do without the friendships and excitements of a normal boy's life.

"My uncle was a tall, thin man, white-haired and wearing the long side-whiskers of the period. He was not a genial companion for a small boy. He was patient with me and taught me my classics conscientiously, but an air of gentle melancholy seemed to pervade his life and he was subject to fits of intense depression. Sometimes in his study he would break off in the middle of a sentence and sit for long periods gazing into the middle distance with a look of infinite sadness on his face. It was not long before I made a discovery that surprised me. He had a horror of death which would have been unnatural in any grown man, but was even more striking in a clergyman, whom one would expect to view such things with equanimity. (My father, a doctor, had held robust common-sense ideas on the subject which contrasted strangely with my uncle's dark preoccupations.) Every time that there was a funeral in the town and the great bell tolled in the cathedral tower, he would stand at his study window and watch the procession of mourners crossing the close. 'It will be my turn soon,' he used to say as he watched the coffin pass – 'my turn soon - one day I shall be summoned.' He always used this circumlocution - he never spoke of dying, but being summoned or fetched. These occurrences were always followed by periods of preoccupied silence.

"My efforts to establish friendly relations with Thomson, the servant, were not n success. He was, I think, the most silent man I have ever known, and moved about his household duties like a ghost. During my first week I made a number of attempts to engage him in conversation, but he did root respond to my overtures. He used to take me to morning service at the cathedral every Saturday. Once on the way back t gave way to a natural fit of childish curiosity, and asked him if he knew the reason for my uncle's moody ways, and I got the reply that my inquisitiveness deserved.

"'Don't expect *me* to discuss the master with you,' he said severely, and added darkly, 'There's some things better not discussed at all. You be a good boy and be thankful for the home he's made for you, and don't worry your head about things that don' t concern you.' After this our relations were on a strictly formal basis.

"'There was another feature of the Canon's conversation which, in retrospect, was strange. Of course ns a small boy it did not strike me as particularly odd, but it did frighten me rather. On Sundays he used to teach me Scripture, and from his exposition of the Bible it was quite plain that the powers of evil and the torments of the damned were to him concrete, literal things. To him the struggle between good and evil assumed a physical aspect, which was far more in tune with medieval thought than that of the nineteenth century. He would solemnly warn me to be on my guard against the wiles of the Prince of Darkness, who was ever lurking at my side, seeking his opportunity to ensnare me and to establish his control over my immortal soul. He spoke of this subject with a burning sincerity, almost as though he were drawing upon his own experience. Indeed, on several occasions he seemed to be on the verge of making some revelation to me, but he always

155

broke off and relapsed into moody silence. His depression used to communicate itself to me, but not for long. The natural animal spirits of childhood would reassert themselves, and I would soon forget my cares as I explored the streams and eaves of the Mendips.

"Two other curious incidents have, I think, a bearing on this story. The first was commonplace enough. We were in the study and were speaking of the cathedral organist. Looking out of the window, I saw the object of our conversation crossing the close, and I made a remark which seemed to be harmless enough - a remark which must he made hundreds of times every day – 'Talk of the devil,' I said, 'there he is.' The effect on my uncle was startling. He called me from the window in a sharp tone that I had never heard him use before. Sitting upright in his chair, he gazed at me for a moment without speaking. He was very pale and obviously labouring under the stress of some violent emotion, but when he spoke his voice was quiet, almost a whisper.

"'You will never use that expression again,' he said, 'the name you spoke is not one to be employed in a meaningless figure of speech.' I expressed my contrition, though I couldn't really see why he was so serious about it. It seemed such a little thing. 'All right,' he said, 'we will say no more about it. I know you spoke in ignorance.' He never referred to the matter again.

"The second incident made an even greater impression on me; sometimes in the evening I used to read to the old man. I was a precocious child and read well in a rather expressionless way. My uncle, I think, liked it. He used to sit with half-closed eyes and listen as I declaimed passages from the English poets. Tennyson was his favourite, and I must have got through the 'Idylls of the King' three or four times. One day I bought at the town bookshop a little anthology of poems and when I was next asked to read I took it up and opened it at random. The piece which I lp>it upon was an extract from Marlowe's 'Doctor Faustus,' and I began; 'Was this the face that launched a thousand ships And burned the topless towers of Ilium…' At this point the book was snatched from my hand and hurled on the floor. My uncle struggled to his feet and his eyes blazed with anger. I was frightened.

"'Where did this book come from?' he demanded. 'Who told you to read this passage to me?'

"'No one told me to,' I faltered. 'I bought it in the town.'

"He flung the book into the fire, and I watched it burn with miserable eyes; then he slumped back into his chair and muttered more to himself than to me 'Dr Faustus, Dr Faustus,' then looking at me, 'Don't worry, child, you didn't know what you wore doing. You're only an instrument sent to remind me.' He gave a mirthless laugh and repeated, 'to remind me - Great God! As though I needed reminding.'

"He rose slowly and went up to his room, and I went up to mine. I heard him limping up and down muttering to himself. I pressed my ear to the wall to try to catch what he was saying, but it was inaudible. Finally, I heard the springs of the bed creak as he lowered himself on to it-then a sound came to my ears that sent a thrill through me. The old man was weeping. The sound of his stifled sobs through the wall terrified me. I had never heard a grown-up weep before. Such a thing was beyond my comprehension.

"The following day he was quite normal again and made no allusion to the event of the previous night, and our life resumed its humdrum plane.

"I should have said before that my uncle had an occupation. He was writing a book. It was a commentary upon the Pauline

Epistles on which, he told me, he had been working for many years. It was in this work that he took his chief pleasure, and to which he turned in his hours of depression as a kind of palliative. I'm sure that he genuinely loved his task and I can see him now, bent over the vast folio of some earlier commentator, carefully making notes on a sheet of foolscap with a quill. He often expressed the hope that the work would be completed 'before he was summoned'. And as he used the phrase his face would cloud over and he would sigh deeply.

"And so I lived for a year in that ecclesiastical backwater not exactly unhappy, for I was of a contented disposition, but often finding myself ill at ease in the presence of my guardian.

"It was in February 1890 that this placid existence was rudely disturbed. It was a wintry afternoon and the sky was dark with snow clouds. The rooks were circling round the trees in the close and, though it was not yet four o'clock, dusk was beginning to fall. I remember that I was reading Homer in the study with my uncle and he was quoting a passage. Suddenly he stopped in the middle of a line. I looked up and saw that he was looking out of the window across the darkening close. He looked ghastly; his face was ashen. He laid his hand on my shoulder and his fingers touched the back of my neck; they were icy cold. With the other hand he pointed out into the gathering gloom.

"'Look,' he said. 'He's come - he's called for me at last. Can't you see him?'

"I peered out between the trees. I thought I saw a shape moving in the dusk, but I could not be certain. My uncle deliberately drew the curtains and made up the fire. He seemed to have mastered himself. He held himself more erect, and the colour returned to his checks. He rang for tea, and we ate the meal in silence. As soon as he had finished he settled down to his favourite work, which had progressed rapidly in the last year and had now reached the Epistle to the Colossians.

"That evening when I went up to bed he took my hand between his. 'God bless you, my child,' he said, 'and may He preserve you from any such act of folly as I myself committed in my youth - an act of folly which has haunted me all my life and for which I shall shortly atone. May you never be tempted, as I was, to have dealings with the Prince of Darkness. For years now I have been waiting for this day, but now that it has come and the expectation and uncertainty is ended, I am strengthened by the thought that my punishment will not be everlasting, for the mercy of God is infinite.'

"I tried to speak, but he dismissed me gently, and my last glimpse of him showed him bending down again over his foolscap sheet, returning, as ever, to the work which had proved his solace for so long.

"I lay awake in my bed, pondering on these strange words, but their implications were beyond my youthful understanding. I listened for the Canon's footsteps on the stairs, but he had not come up to his room before I fell asleep.

"I awoke on the following rooming with a feeling of foreboding, and I tiptoed to my uncle's door and gently opened it. He was not there, nor had his bed been slept in. I ran hastily down to the study and drew the curtains. The room was empty. I quickly roused Thomson, and together we searched every room in the old house. The cripple who had not gone out of doors for years had disappeared. The servant was more taciturn than ever. He left me alone, saying curtly that he was going to make enquiries. Halfway through the morning the Archdeacon's wife came and took me back to her house, where I spent a miserable day. At lunch-time a report came in that at about midnight my uncle had been seen walking through the town - *without his sticks*. At least, the observer, a policeman, had thought it was the Canon, but on reflection he'd dismissed the idea as ridiculous, knowing that the old man was paralysed. At seven in the evening my suspense was ended by the Archdeacon's wife telling me that my uncle had met with a fatal accident. I heard later that his body had been found in a quarry high on the hillside, though how a cripple had managed to scale the rough slope that led to it no one could say.

"You can imagine the sensation that the affair made in the small town. The Archdeacon asked me to stay with him until my future could be settled, and I thankfully accepted. I went across to the old house to fetch some clothes and other small possessions, and for the last time I entered the study where I had left my dead guardian only twenty-four hours before. On the desk lay a sheet of foolscap on which he had been writing. As I looked at it something caught my eye. Below my uncle's neat, regular handwriting had been added another paragraph, in a bold, hard hand, quite unlike that of the old man. It was written in red ink, or so I thought at the time, though later another possibility occurred to me. I read the words there, but their full significance was not made clear to me until I was several years older. The Canon had been annotating Col. i. 13, and below his notes had been written a blasphemous inversion of the verse;

'He hath delivered us from the Kingdom of His dear
Son
and hath translated us to the Power of Darkness.'"

Printed in Great Britain
by Amazon

19077410R00098